PUFFIN BOOKS

My Family and Other Natural Disasters

Josephine Feeney was born and brought up in Leicester, as one of eight children born to Irish parents who had migrated to England during the Second World War. She worked for six years as an English teacher in comprehensive schools in Hull and Rotherham, further specializing to teach children with special needs in Mansfield and Basildon schools, before leaving teaching in 1991 to pursue her writing career full time. Her play, *Dear Tractor*, has been broadcast on Radio Four.

My Family and Other Natural Disasters

Josephine Feeney

PUFFIN BOOKS

For my mother, Anne
and in memory of
my father, Roger

PUFFIN BOOKS

Published by the Penguin Group
Penguin Books Ltd, 27 Wrights Lane, London W8 5TZ, England
Penguin Books USA Inc., 375 Hudson Street, New York, New York 10014, USA
Penguin Books Australia Ltd, Ringwood, Victoria, Australia
Penguin Books Canada Ltd, 10 Alcorn Avenue, Toronto, Ontario, Canada M4V 3B2
Penguin Books (NZ) Ltd, 182–190 Wairau Road, Auckland 10, New Zealand

Penguin Books Ltd, Registered Offices: Harmondsworth, Middlesex, England

First published by Viking 1994
Published in Puffin Books 1995
3 5 7 9 10 8 6 4

Printed in England by Clays Ltd, St Ives plc

CONTENTS

1

WRITING MY LIFE STORY

When you're in trouble, teachers make you sit in a room, facing their personal messages and family photos. Then they shuffle through papers in a file with your name on. These include those letters from your mum about your sore throat or an attack of diarrhoea (spelt in fifteen different ways). There's a note from a teacher about how obstinate or insolent you've been, your vaccination record, and an emergency number to ring (to contact your parent(s) or guardian) if you're savaged by a dog in the playground.

These files are a catalogue of all the things you've done wrong. Not just in the last few weeks – they stretch back to when you were four or five. They're supposed to be your life story. They're not. They just tell the story of why you haven't come to school and why you're not behaving at school. That's not a life story. Sometimes teachers – well, all adults really – don't look for good things. It's like our medical cards. They just say what's been up with us, like measles or mumps. They don't say anything about how healthy we may have been. Our school files just say what we've done wrong. Well, that's not a life story.

HOLY FAMILY SCHOOL · LANGDON · ESSEX

ENGLISH DEPARTMENT

Major Assignment

Title of Assignment: My Life Story

Details: Ask your parents and grandparents (wherever possible) for details about your early life. They might also be willing to tell you about *their* early life: for example, if your grandparents or parents were immigrants, a little about their homeland and how they came to live in this country. You can include amusing/interesting stories about your early childhood.

Submission Date: 7 June

My Life Story

BY DARREN PATRICK CONNOLLY

I was born in Langdon, Essex, on 14 July, almost fourteen years ago. There was some disagreement over my name. My mother and father wanted to call me Darren because they liked it and, at the time, it was a fashionable name. Then, the day before the christening, my grandmother objected to my name. She said it wasn't a proper Christian name and that my parents were acting like heathens calling me such a name. She also said that the priest wouldn't baptize me if I was called Darren. So at the last minute my parents added the name Patrick, to please my grandmother. Since then she has always called me Patrick or Patsy or just Pat. My mother and father have called me Patrick in the last couple of years because they felt that I may have a split personality if I was called two different names. So, there you are: Darren Patrick Connolly.

That's about all I can think of. I haven't got much of a life story. Well, I'm only thirteen, nearly fourteen – that's not really a lifetime, is it?

Oh yes, there *is* something else. I'm an only child. My parents are called Kathleen and Sean.

THE END

HOLY FAMILY SCHOOL · LANGDON · ESSEX

Mrs K. Connolly
24 Lansbury Gardens
Langdon
Essex

10 June

Dear Mrs Connolly

I regret to inform you that Darren failed to complete his major English assignment by the given deadline. As Darren prepares for the important exams at the end of year eleven, it is vitally important that he completes each assignment on time.

Darren's work did not meet the minimum requirements for this assignment, therefore I feel that it would be in his best interests if he was detained after school next Friday to complete this work. If you have any objections to this course of action, please contact me at the earliest opportunity.

Yours sincerely

J. J. Murphy

J.J.Murphy
Deputy Headteacher

The detention room is like a greenhouse. No windows open, just glass letting the June heat toast the detainee. This room has been specially chosen. Well, that's what Anthony Dunn says, and he seems to know. The teachers got together around their ashtrays and mucky coffee cups and asked one another, in menacing voices, 'Which is the most uncomfortable room in the school?' They chose the one room everyone passes on their way out. The room where everyone looks on a Friday afternoon to see who's been kept behind. The room where it's freezing in winter and boiling in summer.

Anthony Dunn, Chris Dixon and me are friends. We're usually in everything together – even detention. But today, I'm here by myself.

I'm all alone in this room with Sister Mary Rita. She seems to be sorting out her credit card slips. It's hard to believe that nuns have credit cards. I wonder what she buys with hers. When she thinks I'm working she looks at me with pity, as if to say, 'Where did we go wrong?' My mother looks at me like that too, when she thinks I'm absorbed in my computer. Sister Mary Rita and my mother both belong to the parish women's group, although my mum doesn't go to many meetings.

When I look up quickly at Sister Mary Rita she smiles slightly and then returns to her calculator and seems to ask herself why she spent so much in Sainsbury's last week. I wonder then again what nuns buy in Sainsbury's. Do they buy beefburgers and oven chips like my mother?

My mother should be sitting here, sweating in

this June heat. Last week I asked her to help me with my latest English assignment. She flipped – she went absolutely mad. We were asked to write our autobiography. I had to find out all about my parents' background. Mother refused. She said the school was too nosy.

'Why, in God's name, do they need to know about your background?' She always brings religion into it when she's angry.

'We've got to write our life stories,' I pleaded.

'You haven't got a life story. You're only thirteen!' She seemed to spit the words at me.

'Mum, I've got thirteen years.' I felt hurt and sort of hollow to think that she didn't consider those thirteen years were a life story. She went really quiet.

'Well, you write your life story. Just keep me out of it.'

I waited a few minutes until she'd really calmed down. I wrote a couple of things down, like my date of birth and where I was born, then I looked up at my mother again. She was sitting gazing at the privet hedge just outside the window. Beyond that was the washing she'd hung out earlier, when she came in from work. She loves watching the washing swaying across our garden. I don't know why she doesn't use the tumble-drier. She rushes every evening to empty the machine and peg out yesterday's clothes. My dad bought her the tumble-drier one Christmas. I think that's why she doesn't use it.

By now she was quiet again. 'Mum,' I started in

my most gentle, I'll-do-anything-if-you-iron-my-shirt voice, 'can I just explain something?'

'All right, but don't be too long. *Coronation Street* is on in a minute.'

The competition was stiff, but I tried. 'In our English lesson today, Murphy . . .'

'Mister Murphy,' she interrupted. If she knew him like I did, she wouldn't insist on him being called 'Mister'.

'Mister Murphy read us an extract from the life of this bloke called John Pilger.' She was miles away, but I struggled on. 'Anyway, John Pilger starts his life story off by telling how his ancestors were transported to Australia from Ireland. They were treated like animals . . .' I was just getting into it when she interrupted me again.

'So, what do you want to know? How your ancestors were transported from the West of Ireland to Dagenham?'

'Yes . . . yes, something like that.' I faltered because I wasn't really sure if she was being sarcastic. 'I just want to know how I came to be here.'

'Patrick.' The way she said my name I was either in for another volume of the facts of life or she was going to say something about my dad. 'Patrick, love, I just can't talk about it at the moment. Can't you explain to Mr Murphy?'

I knew it. I knew it. It was to do with my dad. She looked out again at the privet and the washing, biting the knuckle joint in her thumb and wishing the tears back up her face. She rocked herself a little and then jumped out of the chair. I heard her walk slowly and desperately up the stairs.

About ten minutes later, above the *Coronation Street* theme tune, I heard her sobbing. She didn't come down again. I brought the washing in and left it on top of the tumble-drier. I pulled out tomorrow's shirt and, as if believing in miracles, put it on the ironing-board.

The next morning the curtains opened at just after seven. 'Morning, Patrick.' My mother had recovered. 'Here's your shirt, and I've just put some toast on for you.'

When I went down to the kitchen my mum was about to leave for work. I handed her my Home-School diary. 'Can I have a note?'

'What for, love?' She was patient, but she had such a short memory.

'About my life story. Will you write a note to Murphy to explain why I haven't done it, please?'

'Mister Murphy!' she corrected me again.

'Mister Murphy. Please, Mum?'

'No. You'll have to explain yourself.' That was the end of it. She'd made me tuna and cucumber sandwiches, ironed my shirt . . . but no note. 'He'll understand – just be honest. Now, be good.' She ruffled my hair, blew me a kiss, and left for the 7.42 to Fenchurch Street.

Murphy didn't understand. I tried to explain, but he

didn't understand. That's why I'm sitting here, in the detention room, watching Sister Mary Rita checking her credit card bill and trying like mad to think of something, anything, to write.

24 Lansbury Gardens
Langdon
Essex

12 June

Dear Mr Murphy

I'm sorry that Patrick didn't complete his homework on time. This is partly my fault as, due to my work pressures, we didn't have time to discuss this assignment.

As you may appreciate, Patrick is going through a bad patch at the moment, so I would ask that he is treated gently. However, I have no objections to him being in detention on Friday. He will be able to finish his work.

Yours sincerely

Kathleen Connolly

Kathleen Connolly

HOLY FAMILY SCHOOL · LANGDON · ESSEX

DETENTION REPORT

PUPILS PRESENT: Patrick Connolly

DATE: Friday 14 June

REPORT: Patrick had to complete an overdue English assignment. He seemed to find it very difficult to get down to any real work. At times I felt he was behaving almost in a disturbed manner in the way he watched me as I was working and the amount of time he just sat gazing out of the window.

Patrick seems to be really unhappy. I've noticed a big change from the little lad who was in my form in Year Seven. I think we ought to see the parents, just in case . . .

Patrick didn't actually write anything, but he says that he's had a good think about things.

TEACHER ON DUTY: Sister Mary Rita

2
SATURDAYS I SEE MY DAD

24 Lansbury Gardens
Langdon

Thursday

Dear Sean

Patrick's been getting into a bit of bother at school. It's nothing serious, but it could develop. Could you have a word with him on Saturday? I'm not too happy about some of the boys he's mixing with at school, but I suppose there isn't much we can do about that. It's a bad time for him to be getting into trouble - next year he'll be starting his exam courses.

Please let me know how you get on with him. I don't want him to think that he can get away with things just because you have moved out.

By the way, I won't be in on Friday evening as I'm going out with some people from the office after work. Patrick says he'll be able to look after himself.

Regards Kate

There was a queue when I reached the ticket-office at Langdon station. I looked around furtively, hoping to avoid any of my class who might be off to see West Ham or Arsenal. Then I remembered that the season had been over for a few weeks. I'd started catching an earlier train to avoid them. I didn't even see Chris Dixon on the way to his Saturday-morning drama class.

The ticket clerk with the bleached blond hair argued with an elderly man over the date on his railcard. 'Look, grandad . . .' he started in a really nasty tone.

'I'm not your grandad, so don't be so cheeky. And I'm not deaf, so you needn't shout.' Under his breath the old man muttered away. Then suddenly he started to shout again.

The raised voices had drawn in those who hung about the station. Even the girl selling flowers moved inside the station door, keeping one eye on her stall and the other on the disagreement.

Tickets and money were exchanged with great discourtesy, and as the old man walked towards the stairs the ticket clerk waved two yellow-tipped fingers for all the station to see. With just one ticket booth open the queue was steadily extending and I looked impatiently at the timetable monitor.

'Can I buy my weekly ticket for next week, please? It's to Hammersmith.' It was a woman who was about the same age as my mother.

'No!' the clerk shouted. 'Get lost! Next please.' The woman almost fainted in disbelief.

As their argument developed, a second clerk

opened another window and shouted, 'Who's next please?' I bought my ticket and then left the booking-hall, disappointed that I was going to miss the second act of the drama.

The old man with the railcard sat on the other end of the red metal seat on the platform. He looked at me sort of hopefully and said, 'Morning.' He seemed quite shaken. After a few minutes he looked at me again. 'Where you off? Highbury? White Hart Lane?' I dreaded this. Old people always talked to me and I never knew what to say. In a minute he'd start on about when men were really men, wore long shorts and played on fields as big as Essex.

'No, I'm going to my grandad's.' I didn't like to say that I was meeting up with my dad. It sort of said everything.

'I'm going to my late wife's grave.'

'Oh,' I said, 'lovely.' I cringed as I said it. He smiled.

'She's buried in Upminster. Lovely spot. I'll neaten up the little plot and then put these flowers in a bit of water. We'll have a little chat and then I'll come back.' I didn't know whether he was talking to himself or to me. He looked across at the Southend-bound platform.

'"Tommy," she said, "bury me in Upminster." So I did. I'm in that cemetery every Saturday morning. Are you still at school, son?'

'Yes, still at school.' It came out as a sort of laughing statement. The old man laughed too.

'Best days of your life. Make the most of it.' He

moved to the edge of the platform as the train crept in and drew to a standstill. 'Enjoy the match!' he shouted, and he unsteadily climbed into a smokers' carriage whilst I walked quickly towards a non-smoking compartment.

My gran was transplanting a row of lettuces when I arrived. She was so preoccupied that I had to walk right up and stand next to her before she noticed me.

'Jeez, your feet are getting awful big.' She addressed my big white trainers. My gran once told me that she dreaded meeting people and hated goodbyes. 'I'm no good at hello and farewell, but in between I can be good value.' She never knew what to say when I arrived. Today she criticized my growing feet, last week it was my new earring. My gran was from the West of Ireland. My dad said she'd never really left.

'Your garden looks good, Gran,' I started.

'Will you give over. Look at those weeds over near the beans, it's a disgrace!' She couldn't take compliments either.

'Gran, it looks all right to me.' I never knew what to say for the best.

'Come on, we'll put the kettle on. You dad's on the phone and Grandad is up throwing coins in the bottomless pool of that old bookie's. The robbers! How's your mother?'

'She's fine.'

'What's she up to today?' Gran looked at me closely.

'I don't know, Gran, she wasn't up when I left the house.' I tried to change the subject. 'Are you sowing any spuds this year?'

'I am not. This soil's no good for them . . . arra . . . they're cheap enough at the old greengrocer's up there on the parade. Why wasn't your mother up? Is she sick?'

'No, I think she's fine. She had a bit of a late night.'

'Did she indeed?' My gran looked up at me as if I was a neglected workhouse child. 'Well, I hope to God you don't turn into one of those juvenile delinquents, with a mother and father like yours.' She put her hand up and stroked the side of my face. 'Ah, sure . . . your Blessed Mother is watching over you all the time. She certainly doesn't work in the City, and she'll protect you from all that magguy-ana.' She pinched my cheek and pushed me towards the house.

'Marijuana, Gran,' I corrected her.

'That an' all!' she laughed, relieved that the moment had passed.

I heard the comforting sound of the kettle being filled, as my gran whistled in the kitchen. In the hall, my dad made arrangements on the phone. I coughed really loudly and then I heard him say, 'I'll have to shoot, I think my boy's here.'

About five years ago my dad retrained as a youth and community worker. Before that he worked at Ford's, training apprentices (he was always good with people). When some of the workers were offered voluntary redundancy, the union agreed to help people find places on college courses so they could retrain for other careers. My dad went to college in London – he used to catch the train every morning, and in the evening he'd come home piled up with books and assignments. Since then he can be a bit embarrassing at times. He picked up funny phrases from the other students at college and he's not as straightforward as he used to be.

'So . . .' He always said that. It meant a thousand things to my dad. This morning he shrugged his shoulders and I knew that meant, 'How are you?'

'Fine, Dad.'

'School?'

'Not bad.' I looked down at the racing pages of the *Mirror*.

'Not bad?'

'Yeah . . . it's OK.' My dad gave me one of his long meaningful looks, trying to pierce through my face to see what I was thinking.

'How are your mates? Dixon and Dunny, is it? They're not leading you into mischief, are they?'

Why do parents always blame your friends?

Gran bustled in from the kitchen with two mugs of tea and placed them in front of me and my dad with a short, sharp, high-pitched, 'Now.' She could always tell when my dad was trying to talk to me.

Gran's sitting-room is dominated by the Sacred Heart picture and the television. In the centre of the room is a coffee-table my dad made at school. The alcove behind the television is full of photos of all the grandchildren. I sat back on the Dralon settee and listened to my dad.

'I had a letter from your mother, Patrick. She said you'd been in trouble at school?' Dad was also really into making statements sound like questions. 'Are you struggling?' Sitting back in his armchair, he took a deep gulp of Gran's tea.

'Do we have to talk about school on Saturday, Dad?' He was the one who always used to say we should shake the dust of work from our shoulders on a Friday evening. I sat further back on the settee and tried to smile the smile that used to produce the train-set from the loft. It didn't really work.

'Yes, you've got a point, Patrick.' My dad, despite all his faults, is quite sensitive. 'If you're having any difficulties, just ring me. I'll help you with anything, son.'

Whilst he was in such a receptive mood, I told him about my autobiography and the detention.

'Murphy doesn't like me, Dad. That's why he put me in detention. It's not really about the assignment. I can't do anything right in his class.'

My dad pushed himself up from the chair and started to walk around the room, past the Sacred Heart picture, the television and the framed grandchildren. 'Why didn't you do your homework, Patrick? You shouldn't be falling behind at this stage.'

'What?' I was furious. It wasn't *my* fault that I couldn't do my homework properly. 'Dad, I can't do my autobiography, that's all. I don't know anything about my ancestors. I don't know anything really about you or Mum. It's not my fault, Dad. Is it? Is it?'

My dad looked stunned. There was no noise coming from the kitchen. I could sense my gran standing still against the workbench, listening intently to where I was going wrong.

'Why didn't you ring me and ask for help?' Dad implored. 'That's what I'm here for.'

I didn't want to ring my dad to ask for help with my school problems. I wanted him to be back home. 'Why don't you come home, so I don't *have* to ring you?' I threw the question across the room. My dad looked as though I'd just slapped him. He walked into the kitchen and then out of the back door.

Gran followed him. He walked up close to where the spring cabbages had been and looked up into the sky as if watching a passing aircraft. Gran stood a short distance away, next to the runner-bean poles. She was carrying a tea-towel, which flapped all over the place as she gave out to my dad. He didn't acknowledge her advice, he just carried on searching the sky before he finally blew his nose. They both went quiet and then looked at the soil. Gran noticed me watching from the window and pulled my dad's sleeve as if telling him to go back into the house.

I'd never seen my dad cry before. It was hard to understand what was happening. Dad sat down on the settee facing the Sacred Heart picture and Gran sat beside him, stroking his hand. 'Patrick,' she began, 'I wonder if you can knock any sense into your father's head. Or your mother's for that matter.' Then, as if to herself, 'Things are made too easy these days . . . and it's always the youngsters who suffer.'

'I didn't mean to upset you, Dad. I'm sorry.'

'It's not your fault, son. You're right, I should be there, but it's not that easy . . . or simple.' He reached over and took my hand. We were like a chain, me, my dad and Gran. 'Patrick, I'll try to help you with your work today. We'll sort Murphy out!'

'Mister Murphy,' I corrected him, imitating my mother. We laughed.

3

MY PARENTS ARE SEPARATED

It's difficult to explain. I still can't understand it properly and it still hurts. My parents are separated. Like my dad's shorthand, that says everything. I don't know what really happened. I've never been told and it sort of happened gradually.

My parents never told me that they were separating. I don't know what happened. I often wish that there was 'another' man or woman whom I could hate. I just have this dull confused feeling in my stomach all the time. I wanted to know, but I was too frightened to ask and so my parents remained silent.

Dad started working in a youth centre near Dagenham, so some nights, when he was working long shifts, he stayed with Gran and Grandad. One week I realized that he hadn't been home at all, so I rang him at Gran's. He said it was easier for him to live there because of his job. Mum cried every night for weeks, when she thought I couldn't hear. Then she suggested that I should meet up with my dad on Saturdays.

One evening I heard my mum talking to her friend on the phone. She was always very guarded, but I did hear her say, 'It's like a long, lingering death.'

I can't talk about it with my friends, Dixon and Dunny, at school. It's not something that you can laugh and joke about. My parents don't mention it. The teachers know. Once I was summoned to talk to the Head of Year – she's the woman who 'deals' with all our problems. She'd heard that my mum and dad had split up. Her office (she wanted us to call it her 'consulting room') had two easy chairs, lots of plants, and posters saying things like, 'A tea-break is God's apostrophe'.

I didn't want to be there, sitting reading daft posters. I wanted to be out on the field with Dixon and Dunny. This was a waste of valuable football time.

'So . . .' she began. Just like my dad. They must have been on a course together. 'You're Darren.'

'I'm Patrick actually, miss.' There was always this confusion.

'Patrick? It says here Darren.' As if you'd pretend to be anyone else in a situation like this. It was like when my Auntie Marian was getting married, the priest called her Marilyn all the way through the ceremony.

'My name is Darren Patrick, but my grandparents don't like the name Darren, so I'm always called by my second name.'

'Oh, I see, Darren. Thanks for explaining that. Now . . . why have you come to see me?'

'You asked me to.'

'Did I?' She looked frantically through her notes. 'Oh yes . . . yes. So . . . how are things with you?'

'Great, thanks.' I looked straight past her at the

second hand moving steadily around the clinical white clock-face.

'Great?' (Which, since my dad has become a youth worker, I have come to learn means 'expand'.)

'Yes, great.' I wasn't telling a lie. Things *had* been quite good at that time.

'And . . . your parents?' She pretended to be preoccupied as she asked, but she looked sharply at my face to register my response. 'Your mother, how is she coping?'

'Very well, thanks.'

'Your father?' She sounded like an American when she spoke these statements as questions.

'He's well. Working hard.'

'But . . .?' She looked at me with a long, heart-searching stare. I wanted just to run out. This wasn't a normal conversation and it certainly wasn't helping me.

'So . . .' (Again!) 'Your parents are no longer living together . . .' She paused as if she'd forgotten her lines.

'No.' I squirmed.

'Do you want to talk about it?' My head sank deeper into the collar of my school shirt. I could almost smell the washing-powder.

'No,' I muttered.

'It might make things better.' She seemed to brighten with the challenge I presented.

Very quietly, I uttered, 'It's none of your business.' Her back straightened and she shuffled her papers.

'Oh, but it *is* my business. That is my job – to listen to all of your problems; to help you out of any difficulties. So . . . tell me, why did your parents split up?'

'I don't know.' Which was the truth, although I wouldn't have told her even if I *had* known.

'Do you feel guilty about it?'

'No!' I almost shouted it at her. It was nothing to do with me, why should I feel guilty?

'How *do* you feel about it? Do you feel angry?' She was so persistent. I just wanted to run out, run to the furthest goalpost, where my mates were aiming shots at Anthony Dunn.

I didn't answer her, but in my mind I kept saying, 'Mind your own business, mind your own bloody business.'

She cleared her throat; her tone changed. 'Your teachers are concerned that it may be affecting your work. So . . . how do you feel about that? Maybe you'd like to talk about it. Has it affected your work?'

'No, miss.'

'No what?' All the sympathy had gone from her voice. She was just like any other teacher now.

'No, I don't want to talk about it, thanks.' I desperately wanted to get out of this room with the plants and the posters. 'Can I go now, miss? I feel sick . . . I think I'm going to be sick.' I put my hand over my mouth and wished my face green.

She moved her body around, out of vomiting range, and then stood up quickly. 'Yes, go. We'll make another appointment.' She opened the door and I left.

I never told my mum or dad about it. On Saturdays my dad just wanted to do something different and exciting and my mum was always too busy to listen.

On this particular Saturday it was warm enough to sit out on the terrace when we reached the Royal Festival Hall. My dad had a way of organizing things when we came into London. We always crossed over from Embankment station for a cup of tea, and then we'd decide where to go. As we crossed Hungerford Bridge he gave money to a few people who were begging. 'It's a short-term solution,' he'd say. He knew some of the people who were homeless, they used to visit his youth centre in Dagenham. Sometimes Dad would invite them to have a coffee or tea with us. Most declined, preferring Dad's ready cash. I was relieved when they just took the money.

As my dad sipped his tea, he watched the juggler on the terrace with a brief smile on his face. Then suddenly he said, 'Listen, Patrick.' I put my head nearer to his over the picnic table. 'I'm going to speak quietly because I don't want everyone to hear.'

After a while he continued. 'Honestly, sometimes I sit here and I overhear other people's lives and . . . well, it's just like bugging a confessional box! No . . . it's just that, your mum and I haven't any great secrets to hide. Maybe . . . when things go wrong, and you haven't worked out why . . . you just find it difficult to talk about the past.'

'Why, Dad?' I was lost. I didn't really understand what he was saying.

'Well . . . you feel that everything you've done over a number of years has been the result of an error of judgement.' Dad looked at me intently. 'Do you understand, Patrick?'

'No, Dad, honest. I don't understand what you're on about.'

'It's so difficult to explain.' He paused, looked at his hands, then at the river. 'Look at it like this. When you meet somebody and fall in love you are so happy . . . that . . . everything seems right, everything seems in tune. Then you marry, have children, and for years you are preoccupied with your family. Then, when things start to go wrong you wonder if you had ever actually been happy. You think that it was just a dream. You even start to think that for all those years everything had been a mistake.' He paused. Then, after a while, 'Do you see?'

'Yes, Dad.' I didn't, but my head started to ache.

'You've gone really quiet, Patrick. Tell me what you're thinking.'

'Am I part of that mistake, Dad?'

'Oh my God, no!' His horror drew attention to our table. People on nearby tables were now listening to *our* lives. 'That's the awful thing. You were the greatest part of our happiness and now, through no fault of your own, you're part of the heartache.'

'What happened, Dad? Why did things change?'

'It's a long story.' Dad watched as the juggler dropped his clubs.

'Will you tell me?' I asked hopefully.

*

We walked along the river past the old GLC building and up to Westminster Bridge. Every time we walked this way we'd stop in the middle and look eastwards, although the view was better from Blackfriars Bridge. As we stood gazing down the river, I realized that my dad probably wouldn't help me at all with my English assignment.

Then – as if he'd read my mind and sensed my doubts – my dad suddenly said that he would try to help me with my English assignment. 'I'll phone your mother this evening and encourage her to help you too.'

'I need to go a bit further back than just you and Mum. What about Gran and Grandad?'

'Ask your gran when we get back today. She might help, but she finds it difficult to talk about her childhood. Things were very difficult for her.'

We walked down Millbank to the Tate Gallery. My dad whistled the tune my gran had been whistling as she had made the tea earlier in the day.

Dagenham

Saturday

Kate

Just a quick note. I've had a word with Patrick today, but we didn't get very far. There are a lot of questions going round in his head and it's difficult for me to answer them all. I'm not sure how much to tell him.

You'll need to help him with his English assignment - help him to get something written down on paper. That seems to be the root of the problem, so if we get this out of the way I think things will run smoothly again.

Did you have a good time with your colleagues on Friday? Glad to hear you're enjoying life!

Be in touch again.

Sean

4

TROUBLE AT SCHOOL

There's only one thing in the world worse than having to go to school – having to go to school when it's raining. I could hear the rain soaking the glass and the window frames, running down the hole in the guttering and diving out from under car tyres.

Rainy schooldays, where the rain searches for the small hole in the hood of your jacket and menacingly trickles down your neck and back; where you delicately balance a notebook on your knee whilst sitting on a bench in the sports hall, trying to write down the rules of rugby.

It was a quarter to eight and there was no movement downstairs. My mother had missed her train. I shouted to her. She leapt out of bed and howled, 'Put the kettle on, Pat!' She ran from wardrobe to cupboard to bathroom and then down the stairs. 'I've just remembered, Patrick, I meant to tell you before. Your dad and I have an appointment with Mr Murphy this morning. He wants to see you too. So . . . don't panic, I've already told the office I'll be late.'

'Shall I catch the school bus or wait for you, Mum?' The day was improving. I might not arrive at school drenched after all, although I was surprised and a little annoyed that my mum hadn't told me about this appointment before.

'Wait for me, Pat. I'm not too sure of the way there.' That shows how many times she'd visited the school.

I couldn't help thinking, Why does Murphy want to see my parents? Why hadn't my mum told me before? Why was I in trouble? The questions were on the tip of my tongue . . . I was really anxious to know what was going on, but I just couldn't ask my mum. I was very confused.

Dad waited in the entrance hall at school. He and Mum greeted one another with the politeness reserved for strangers. Mum looked past Dad's shoulder whilst Dad looked sympathetically into Mum's face. She could have been one of his homeless youths.

'How're things, Sean?' Mum really made an effort, but it was too businesslike to touch my dad at all.

'Fine. You?'

'Not too bad. I'll be pleased when all this is sorted out.' She nodded over towards me.

I stood a safe distance away from my parents – safe enough to disown them if they started arguing violently and close enough to listen if necessary.

Murphy walked up to us and introduced himself to my parents. He gushed, like he did when the headmistress walked into his classroom. We followed him to a small office. Murphy sat behind the large desk in front of the window. He invited my parents to sit the other side of the desk. It reminded me of the Mortgage Enquiries desk in the building society.

'Tea, coffee?' Murphy raised his arms in a continental manner as if inviting them to join him in a *cappuccino*.

'I'd love a cup of tea, please. No sugar, thanks.' My mother settled herself into her chair.

'Black coffee for me, please,' Dad replied.

'Sugar?' I had never seen Murphy being so polite.

'No, no. Just black.'

'Patrick, would you like to take our order along to Mrs Mullaney and then wait in the reception area until you're summoned.' Murphy smiled as he ordered me out of the room. I never realized he had any smiling muscles in his face. He seemed to reserve his smiles for other teachers and parents. When Murphy was being sarcastic, he tried to smile, but you could see it wasn't genuine.

At times it was hard to believe that Murphy had our 'best interests' at heart – he never listened when we tried to explain our difficulties. 'No excuses!' he shouted, as we presented a variety of reasons for not doing homework.

I sat and waited in the reception area – as conspicuous as a broken pane in a greenhouse. The latecomers trooped in drenched and full of original excuses for oversleeping. The school office was full of activity and scandal. I heard Mrs Mullaney say 'Never!' about twenty times. The phone rang constantly. Sister Mary Rita walked past, winked at me and half shouted, 'Hope you get the job!'

Messages came and went, borne by a variety of carriers. Some stared at me as if watching to see if I'd move whilst waiting for their replies. Chris Dixon arrived late, equipped only with his leather football. At first he didn't notice me, then suddenly he shouted, 'Hey, Damp Proof Course!' I'd been called that ever since one economics lesson when we'd looked at brochures for selling houses. My initials are D. P. C. – Darren Patrick Connolly. 'Damp Proof Course' just stuck. Still, it was better than gas-fired central heating.

Chris walked over. 'What you doing here, you skiver?'

'Murphy's with my parents.'

'You been bad?' Chris was an expert at short sentences and understatements.

'Slightly,' I said, with some pride.

Chris didn't notice Murphy walking up behind him. 'I hate Murphy. He's a right bigoted . . .' He would have continued, but he noticed my anxious expression as I moved my head purposefully.

'And I was never keen on you, Dixon. Clear off back to class, will you. It's in your own best interests!' Murphy seemed irritated.

I thought Chris would collapse. 'I didn't mean you, sir. I meant Dermot Murphy in 11G. I hate the way . . .' Once again Murphy prevented Chris from finishing a sentence.

'Go away, Dixon. You're just digging an enormous hole for yourself. If it helps your conscience, I won't lose any sleep over the fact that you hate me. Do you feel better now?' Murphy's red anger contrasted sharply with his crisp white shirt. 'Connolly, get back in there with your parents.'

I walked slowly and deliberately along the corridor, past all the Technology Attainment Target Three display work, as if these were my last few steps before the scaffold. My parents were quiet when I walked into the room. My father looked desperately towards my mother, who, in turn, fixed her eyes on a tear-sodden tissue which she was holding. The rainy-schoolday-morning feeling hit me cruelly as I saw my mother sitting there looking so unhappy. Murphy did all the talking. I didn't hear a word he said. My eyes were fixed firmly on my mother as she wrung the usefulness from the tissue. As she blew her nose and dabbed her eyes I noticed, for the first time, that she was no longer wearing her wedding ring.

I had been suspended from school for two days – specifically, so Murphy said, to 'sort myself out'. Dad, Mum and I returned home. Dad informed Mum's work that she was unwell. Then he rang the youth centre and said something urgent had cropped up.

We were all back together momentarily. This is not how I imagined it would be. It felt as though someone had ripped a few pages from the middle of a storybook. You know all the characters, but you're not sure what's happening because that big chunk is missing. We didn't know what to say to one another. I walked out to the kitchen, put the kettle on and then watched raindrops running down the window, avoiding one another, meeting up, joining forces and eventually crashing into the window-sill.

'Who wants tea?' I shouted. As my gran says, 'There's nothing gets people talking quicker than putting salad cream in banana sandwiches.'

'Patrick, you come in here and I'll sort out the tea.' It was my dad. 'Your mother wants to talk to you, now.' Dad and I swapped places. Mum had recovered slightly. She opened her handbag and took out a long buff envelope.

'Whilst your father's here you can read this, Patrick.' She threw the letter at me whilst staring smugly at my dad. 'Then we'll try to sort out this mess . . . all together!'

As I read she stared at the top of my head as if checking the neatness of my parting. I couldn't understand why she hadn't shown the letter to me before. It was from school.

HOLY FAMILY SCHOOL · LANGDON · ESSEX

Mrs K. Connolly
24 Lansbury Gardens
Langdon
Essex

17 June

Dear Mrs Connolly

I am writing to you today because I am very concerned about your son, Darren.

Over the last few months there has been a marked change in Darren's attitude and behaviour. Several teachers have spoken to me recently concerning Darren's approach to his work. At a recent staff meeting the following points were brought to my attention concerning Darren:

1. Darren has flatly refused to complete an English assignment on his life story;
2. When questioned about this Darren claimed that it was a means for the school to pry into his home life;
3. As a result of this episode Darren was detained after school. In the detention he completed no work and, according to the teacher on duty, spent most of his time 'looking out of the window'.
4. When it came to our attention that Darren's home circumstances had changed, Darren was given the opportunity to talk to

his Head of Year (who has attended many counselling courses). She reports that Darren was extremely rude, saying that his difficulties were none of her business. He also told this teacher that he would 'be sick' if he wasn't allowed to leave the room.

We feel that Darren is an intelligent young man with considerable potential. However, if he continues to display such disturbed behaviour he may well wreck his chances of future success. In an age of increasing competition this would be most regrettable.

Would you please contact the school at your earliest opportunity to arrange an appointment so that we may discuss Darren's future.

I look forward to hearing from you.

Yours sincerely

John J. Murphy

J.J. Murphy
Deputy Headteacher

I felt as though I was looking at my reflection in a shop window and seeing a stranger. Everything in the room seemed to be different. The furniture, pictures, carpets were as if they had been replaced in the last few minutes. I didn't know what to say. Murphy wasn't lying – everything in the letter was true, but it was exaggerated. I didn't know what to say. My parents' eyes hovered over me, impatient for a response.

'Patrick there's no excuse for such rudeness. I've always taught you to be polite and well-mannered. I'm really ashamed . . . especially after talking to Mr Murphy this morning!' My mother was furious.

'Don't be so harsh, Kate. We haven't heard what Patrick's got to say.' Dad was angry too, but in a different way.

'It doesn't matter what Patrick's got to say. There's no excuse . . . he shouldn't have been rude. I don't care what the teachers are like, you should be polite to all of them.' There was a pleading tone in her voice.

'Well, I don't agree with that. Why should he be polite to someone who's nasty and vindictive? He doesn't have to tug his forelock to these people. Some of these teachers need to earn respect.'

'Patrick was rude. That's the end of it. There are no excuses for being rude and impolite.'

'He's been through a tough time lately, Kate. It's bound to come out in some way.'

'Tough time?' My mum was furious. She marched around the room. 'Call this a tough time?' She gesticulated around the room. 'He's got absolutely everything he needs here. And please don't talk to me about tough times, Sean. That's still no excuse.'

'It's just as well we don't live in the same house any more, with such fundamentally different ideas about parenting.' My dad had a resigned air about him.

'That's right, throw your bloody jargon at me again. Sean, this isn't a case conference, we're not in your youth centre and I'm not one of your bloody clients. So for a few minutes would you mind acting as a responsible father rather than a play leader!'

Mum's words, like a burst bag of nails, reached into all corners of the room. Dad stood up and walked towards the door. 'I'm going, Kate. See you Saturday, Patrick.'

'What?' Mum walked over to the door as if to bar his way. 'Where are you going?'

'Back to work.'

'But we haven't sorted anything out.'

'No, and we're not getting anywhere because I'm just a "play leader". We're just going back over the same old ground and we're not getting anywhere. I may as well go back to my "play schemes", as you always call them.' Dad went to open the back door.

'Please wait, Sean. We both need to talk to Patrick. Just wait a few minutes. I'll sort out some lunch.'

'There's no point, Kate. I'll see Patrick on Saturday.'

'Please.' She meant it. She was really pleading. 'Don't walk out. I can't handle this on my own.' Mum walked slowly back into the room.

I didn't want to be around any more. Their shouting and baiting was nothing to do with me. I didn't need sorting out. It was plain and simple. Murphy had told lies about me – well, exaggerated – and now there was all this fuss. It was so uncomfortable, listening to Mum pleading with Dad to stay. I couldn't take any more, so I slipped quietly out of the back door.

5

LISTENING TO GRAN

The park was empty and the swings moved desolately in the post-rain breeze. At one end was an unofficial community notice, painted on the gable end of somebody's house: 'Dog owners – please don't let your dog mess on the grass. Children play here!'

I sat on one end of a large metal caterpillar, which smiled eternally at the roundabout. I looked around – as I did most evenings – for Dixon and Dunny, forgetting they were securely trapped in school. We always used the white painted notice for our goal – until the house-owners came out and complained about the noise. That was Dixon's fault – he was forever thumping the ball at the notice, almost as though it annoyed him.

I thought about how such a big fuss had been made over a small thing. Clichés like 'storm in a teacup' and 'mountains out of molehills' ran in and out of my brain. My gran hated clichés. She said they were, like swearing, a lazy use of the English language. 'Sure the English never learned how to use their own language properly. They always talk in ready-made sayings.' Gran believed that most people took a stock of phrases down off the shelf every morning and, depending on the weather, used a certain batch. That's what I needed to do, talk to somebody who didn't have ready-made phrases or instant grudges.

Halfway along Gran's street I could hear the horses moving into the stalls and then, as they emptied out, Grandad shouting at the one he had backed. The neighbours seemed to tolerate live commentaries from Goodwood, Redcar, Aintree and Newmarket. Grandad wouldn't wear his hearing-aid.

The kitchen door was open and Gran was just at the side of the house, sorting out the window-boxes. 'Hello, Gran.' I didn't want to frighten her. It was all right creeping up on her on a Saturday, when I was expected.

'Did you forget something last Saturday? Is that why you're here?' She looked at me closely. Grandad's horse must have won; I heard him shouting, 'Good on yer!'

'No, Gran. I just wanted to get out of the house for a while.' She stood quietly in her outsized wellingtons and gardening gloves for just a moment, then returned to her window-boxes.

'Well, I'll tell you what, Patsy. We'll have a nice cup of tea and then you can help me sort out these window-boxes and hanging-baskets. I'm glad you came; you'll be a great help.'

The tea, and banana sandwiches (without salad cream), made me feel better almost instantly. Grandad came out to the kitchen, looking for a box of matches. 'Well, if it isn't himself! Will you watch the next race with me, Patrick?'

The sitting-room was stuffy and misty with cigarette smoke as we waited for the next race. The curtains were closed, to keep the glare from the television. 'How's things?' my grandad asked, without taking his eyes away from the paddock.

'Not bad.' I picked up the paper and looked through his selection.

'Have you a holiday today?' He searched for the matches my gran had given him. 'Sure every day is a holiday when you're at school. Isn't that right?' His lips clutched on to the cigarette as his shoulders shook with the delight of his own joke. 'Did you know I went to a high school, Patrick?'

'Did you, Grandad?' I'd heard the joke before but still I supplied the necessary response.

'I did. One on top of a hill!' Again he laughed, cleverly balancing the cigarette on the edge of his smiling mouth. He leaned forward; the race was about to begin. 'Quiet now. I'm on to a winner here.'

In the middle of the race Gran called out to me, much to Grandad's annoyance. 'Will you leave the boy alone for a minute whilst we watch my horse win,' he grumbled.

'You'd be a bad influence on the Divil himself.' Gran had marched in and stood to one side of the television. Grandad held out one hand weakly, bidding Gran to stay where she was. Then the hypnotic frenzy of the commentator's voice and the pounding hoofs drew Gran into the race.

Grandad had a winner at three to one. He punched the air and kissed Gran and myself as he celebrated. 'You can buy some tomato plants with those winnings, me boyo!' Gran, ever practical, reminded him of his responsibilities to the greenhouse in the back garden.

Wearing some of my dad's old clothes, I filled up the window-boxes with compost. Gran brought out the trays of annuals from the greenhouse and set them before me with a detailed explanation about each one.

'Marigolds are fierce easy to grow, so I have plenty of these. These nasturtiums drape down beautifully, so we'll put a few of those in the edges of each one.' Then, after a while, as I levelled out the compost, 'Why aren't you at school today, Patrick?'

'I've been suspended.'

'Why?'

I told her the whole story. She didn't look at me at all, but sprinkled some sort of fibre on to the window-boxes.

'Where are your parents now?'

'They were arguing, so I just walked out. It isn't really anything to do with me.'

Gran passed three geraniums. 'Put these in the middle of each box. They make a good centre. Why didn't you do your work in the first place? Isn't that where it all started?'

'I didn't know what to write.' I seemed to be repeating myself so much lately.

'Couldn't you make it up? Your dad used to be

really good at writing stories. We'll get some lobelia out of the greenhouse to put around the edges of this box here.' Gran always had a short, simple answer to even the most complex of problems.

'Would you tell me your life story, Gran?' She looked at me as if I'd said something really stupid. I tried to convince her. 'It would be a great help.'

'I will, of course, but there isn't much to tell.'

'You must have loads to tell – sixty-six exciting years!'

Gran laughed. 'Right so, I'll tell you, but it isn't all that interesting.' She emptied several plants from their containers as she spoke. 'Let me see now.' She paused. 'I was born in 1925 in Mayo, close to Charlestown. Second of eight children. My father was a farmer; weren't all the men? Women didn't go out to work in those days, and wasn't the world a better place? So . . . my mother was always around the house. I came to England in 1944. The British came over to recruit Irish workers during the war. Worked in hospital kitchens, then school kitchens in the early 1950s. Met old "Lester Piggott" in there –' she nodded towards the house – 'in 1953 at a parish dance. Married himself later that year. Sean was born in 1954, followed by Marian a year later and Teresa, 1961. That's it really, nothing much else to say.'

'What about all the things that have happened since 1961, Gran?'

'Ah sure, they haven't happened to me, they happened to other people. The kids started school when they were five. Sean went off to Ford's, Marian went off to university and Teresa into nursing. Then they married, had their own children, and here we are now.'

'What about when you were young, Gran?' I needed a little more than this for my assignment.

'Do you mean when I was a child – like your age?'

'No, younger. What about going to school and all that?' Gran put her trowel down and sat back on her wellingtons.

'Well now, the schoolroom was about a mile away from our house. I used to walk down along with my brothers and sisters. Honest to God, we used to laugh and joke that much. You may not believe this now, but in the summer we didn't wear any shoes at all. We knew it was summer when we could kick off the old boots. What a sweet day that was.' Gran looked past the window-boxes, hanging-baskets and vegetables. She looked beyond Dagenham. 'God be with those days.' She jumped up quickly and placed a completed window-box on a window-sill.

'Do you miss Ireland, Gran?' There were so many questions I wanted to ask. Wiping her eyes with the back of her gardening glove, she knelt down again over a window-box set with only two fuchsia plants.

'Do you know, Patrick, in the west of Ireland, fuchsias grow wild on bushes along the road. You wouldn't have to buy any plants at all. They call them the tears of Christ. Do I miss Ireland?' She repeated my question. 'It's awful hard to say. I've lived here more years than I lived in Mayo, but . . . all the same, that's my homeland. When I first came I missed home, oh, I missed it so much. Then . . . I sort of got used to this place. When you have your children, things are very, very different.'

'How do you mean, Gran?'

'When your children are born in a place you sort of belong to that place. I wasn't an outsider any longer, I felt more . . . I suppose you could say that I felt more at home. Then, in Dagenham anyway, every other one you met was from Cork. There were times when you felt you were in Ireland!' Gran laughed and rubbed her gardening gloves together. 'C'mon, Patrick, let's get down to work. Is that any help to you at all?'

'Yes, sort of. What about my dad?'

'Now, what do you want to know about your dad that you don't already know?'

'I don't feel as though I know very much about my dad, Gran.'

'Do you know, Patrick, I sometimes have the same feeling myself.' As Gran carried out the tray of busy Lizzies from the greenhouse, I listened to her talking about my dad. I felt confident that this evening I'd be able to write the first part of my autobiography. I could see it written down. At last I had something interesting to write.

32 Poplar Crescent
Dagenham

Thursday evening

Dear Kate

Would yourself and Sean just spend a few minutes talking to your son. He's been here today, helped me with the gardening. If you're not careful, he'll go off the rails. What the hell are you two playing at? Patrick's the one who'll suffer. Mark my words.

God bless.

Gran

PS And why are you letting him take time off school? It's not the holidays yet, is it?

6
BACK HOME

'Where the bloody hell have you been? Your father and I have been all over looking for you.' My mother was furious.

'I've been to my gran's.'

'We're here trying to sort out things for you and you run away to your gran's. I'm that angry, Patrick, I could hit you.'

'Patrick . . .' My dad, cool and calm, ever the voice of reason. 'Don't you think we're concerned enough without you running off too?'

'I'm sorry.' I wasn't really, but saying it helped them. 'I wanted to talk to Gran.'

'Don't you want to talk to us, Patrick?' My dad's measured voice covered his anger, though not completely.

'Yes . . . but you've enough on your plate.' I wanted them to sort out their differences. 'I'm going up to do my homework now.'

'Patrick!' My mother, raging, bellowed at me as I tried to leave the room. 'Get in here! We need to talk. Sit down on that settee and don't move until we've finished. Do you hear?'

'Yes, Mum . . . Dad.' The liberal parents had gone. Maybe they had taken lessons from Murphy. For an hour we talked. They tried to explain why they were no longer living together, but I didn't understand. It had been a funny day.

I didn't go up to my room that evening. My dad and I cooked our standard tea – sausage, bacon, beans and spuds – just to give my mum a break.

I was allowed out after tea. I met up with Chris Dixon and his leather football in the dog-free park. Anthony Dunn wandered over after a while and demanded to be in goal for our kick-about. Chris Dixon said it was his ball and he should go in goal first. Otherwise he'd go back indoors and take his ball with him. Dunny conceded. Our kick-abouts always started like this, arguing about who should do what.

After a while, as there were only three of us, we were really just aiming shots at Dunny. Dunny was a headcase when it came to being a goalie. He would have dived into a vat of molten lava if it stopped the ball going into the net. He'd jump on your feet even if you were wearing running spikes. I liked Dunny. He lived for football and nothing else. All the girls liked him, but he used to say, 'I'm not letting anything interfere with my football career.' His Saturday league team had given him a bravery award three years running because of all the bones he'd broken in the course of duty.

Dixon was another matter. He loved having a kick-around, but his Saturdays were taken up with a drama group. I once asked him if I could join, but he said you had to be referred by the child psychologist. They had said that it was only for 'troubled' children. Dixon didn't mind being called that. It's amazing – if you get into a lot of trouble at school you seem to be given all sorts of perks like that.

My mother liked Anthony Dunn, but she didn't like me being friends with Dixon. I could never bring him home because she said he was light-fingered. He couldn't have taken anything from our house without us noticing. I mean, if he tried to take the microwave out of the front door, you'd see him and you'd just say, 'Put that back, Chris, we need it for our dinner.' My mother said that wasn't the point. She said he had links with the 'criminal subculture', and although he might not actually steal himself, he could tell burglars what was available in our house. Apart from my computer, there was nothing in our house worth nicking.

Dixon and Dunny wanted to know all about my suspension. We sat in a row on the smiling caterpillar and I told them all about Murphy – in particular, the lies he had told in the letter. Dunny spat viciously at the ground and said, 'I hate that man!' His actions and words spoke loudly for all three of us.

'He said I've got to use these two days, whilst I'm suspended, to sort myself out.' Dixon and Dunny tutted in the right places and rolled their eyes as if afflicted by some mental condition.

'Murphy once suspended me so that I could "get my act together", as if I was a comedian or something.' Dixon half laughed as he told us. 'He kept saying, "It's in your own best interests." Rubbish! He just wanted me out of the way for a couple of days.'

'He talks like someone out of an Australian soap!

Normal people don't say things like he does!' We laughed at Dunny's remark.

It was true. Murphy often seemed like a cross between an American oil executive and a harassed police detective on a difficult case. He had a set of stock phrases which he used when dealing with difficult cases. He was the most widely impersonated teacher in the school – his predictability was a gift for those searching for easy laughs.

When I arrived home, the lounge was lit, as usual, by two small lamps throwing oval shadows on to the wall. On the table a busy Lizzie plant reached out proudly and confidently towards the picture of the Spanish Arch on Claddagh Quay in Galway. There was a note from my dad on the table:

Dear Patrick

Your mother is unwell. She's not going to work in the morning, so don't waken her. I've gone back to Gran's tonight, but I'm coming here again tomorrow. We'll talk.

Must shoot.

Dad

Dad had chosen his words so carefully. He hadn't mentioned home. Gran's wasn't home and our house was just 'here'. Murphy said *I* needed sorting out, but my dad didn't even know where *he* was.

7

A FEW DAYS' BREAK

24 Lansbury Gardens
Langdon
Essex

21 June

Dear Mr Murphy

First of all I'd like to thank you for the time you spent with us yesterday. Patrick's father and I are grateful for your patience and kindness in dealing with Patrick.

Patrick is going through a difficult time in his life at the moment, so I am taking him to Ireland for a few days to give him a break from the situation.

He will be back in school on Monday 1 July. I will make sure that he catches up on any work that has been missed.

Yours sincerely

Kate Connolly

Kathleen Connolly

24 Lansbury Gardens
Langdon
Essex

21 June

Dear Sister Mary Rita

Just a quick note to let you know that I won't be able to attend the Women's Group get-together next Saturday. I'm sorry about this. I realize you're hoping for a good attendance for your guest speaker. The thing is, Patrick and I are going away for a few days - we both need a break! We're going to stay with some of my relations in Ireland.

Hope the meeting goes well.

Yours sincerely

Kate Connolly

Kate Connolly

My parents decided that it would be good for me to have a break away from everything. I would have enjoyed Florida or Alton Towers. Instead we headed for Dun Laoghaire.

My mother and I sat next to a Dublin woman who deified the Royal Family most of the way across the Irish Sea. My mother, never a great royalist, bore it for a while in silence, then: 'Don't you think it's scandalous that the Queen spends a fortune each year on clothes?'

'Sure isn't it a great investment?' the Dublin woman retorted.

'It would be better invested in the National Health Service or education!' My mother was stony-faced and ready for a long argument.

'Well now, I've heard that the Queen really lifts people's spirits when she visits a place. Aren't the clothes worth that at least?'

'People's spirits are lifted when they see a good situation comedy on television, or a pantomime,' my mother said, showing the depths of her cultural experience as ever.

'Well, that's an awful thing to say. How can you possibly compare the Queen to a pantomime?'

'That's exactly my point. They're like a year-long pantomime. The royals are just well-known faces promoting British products at a tremendous cost to the British taxpayer!'

People around were beginning to listen in, and some started their own little discussions, as if a teacher had told them to go away and discuss in pairs.

'Sure Ireland has its own royalty,' shouted one man, whose mouth was never far from the small flask he was carrying.

'What?' The Dublin woman looked towards him impatiently.

'King Jackie of Italy!' the man roared, and all around him laughed at his wit. The Dublin woman looked angrily at my mother.

'If Ireland had a royal family itself, the likes of him would have a bit more class!'

'Who?' the man with the flask goaded her. 'Jackie Charlton? Sure Jack is the finest king of all Ireland. That's class for you, Missis.' He raised the flask as if to say cheers, and winked at the Dublin woman. She replied with a look that would have silenced a sober man.

My mother seemed to be different. She smiled as she argued her anti-royal case. We hadn't been on our journey long before I noticed a big change in her attitude. I don't know what my mum and dad had talked about when I was in the park with Dixon and Dunny, but my mum seemed to be better already.

As my mum debated with the other travellers, I started to think about what had happened over the last few days. My dad did come back the following evening and we did talk. Well, they talked – I listened. I'd heard much of it before:

'We love you just as much . . .'
'We just can't live together any more . . .'
'We know it's hard for you to understand . . .'
'Bear with us . . .'
'We want the best for you, son . . .'
'This isn't easy for any of us . . .'
'Things have changed so much . . .'
'Life is so complicated nowadays . . .'

At the end of it all my dad said, 'Well, son?'

Then, after a painful pause, 'Tell us how you feel about all that.'

If somebody hits you across the face really hard so that your eyes water and your cheeks feel swollen and then says 'Tell me how you feel', you never say, 'Terrible.'

'Fine thanks, Dad.' I gave them what they wanted to hear.

I really wanted to scream out, 'Why?' and, 'When you say you can't live together any more does that mean for ever and ever?' It was my fault they didn't tell me. My fault. I never asked the right questions at the right time. I wasn't sure what to ask. It was my own fault they didn't tell me.

A few weeks before Dad had disappeared from the house, Mum decided to redecorate the front room. One of the walls was covered with pictures of us. First Mum and Dad, then the three of us. As she prepared the walls for papering, the photos were taken down, wrapped in old newspaper and put away, next to the train-set in the loft. When the train-set and the Lego had been put away I had felt as though my parents were saying, 'That part of your life is over now – we'll put these up here until . . .'

As I lay in my sleeping-bag on a boat approaching Dun Laoghaire, I wondered if the boxes of photos would ever be brought down. Or if, in years to come, people might unpack the boxes and say, 'Look at this happy, smiling family,' never knowing the rest of the story.

There was a strange stillness on the boat. People had stopped wandering about, the heated discussions had fizzled out and it was mainly silent, though there was a lot of snoring and words spoken from sleep. Underneath it all was the gentle humming of the boat gliding across the still sea. In her sleep my mother lurched towards the Dublin woman. I wished my dad was here, sitting where the Dublin woman was sitting – with Mum's head resting on his shoulder.

24 Lansbury Gardens
Langdon
Essex

21 June

Dear Jim and Sarah

Hope you are in good form. Thanks for the offer of accommodation - I'm really looking forward to seeing my long-lost cousins again!

This is just to confirm that Patrick and I will be arriving in Cork at around midday on Monday. We'll be catching the overnight ferry from Holyhead - docking in Dun Laoghaire at about seven o'clock. I think there's a train for Cork from Dublin at nine.

We'll take a taxi from the station as arranged.
Thanks again for your kindness. See you soon.

Kate

8

CORK CITY

POST CARD

Dear Gran and Grandad
Having a few days' break away from it all in Cork. The weather is sunny and very warm. It's good to be back in the old country! Patrick is on really good form – asking lots of questions about his ancestors! Thanks for your note last week. Don't worry – things are looking better already.
Love, Kate & Patrick

Mr & Mrs Connolly
32 Poplar Crescent
Dagenham
Essex
UK

As we walked into the church in Cork City a woman sat to one side of the door as if collecting the entrance money. She balanced a small child and the two ends of her woollen shawl in one hand and stretched the other out to the entering multitude.

'I've no food for my baby. Spare me a few bob. I'll pray for ye.'

I looked at my mum to see how much we should give, but she pulled me towards the centre aisle of the church.

'Don't you dare!' she hissed. 'It only encourages them.'

'But it's not for her, it's for her baby,' I pleaded.

'Don't be so gullible, Patrick. It's probably to support her heroin habit.'

I looked back at the woman and child with the woollen shawl and thought of my dad. When I glanced back a second time the woman had gone. An elderly priest stood close to where she had been, rubbing his hands as if he'd just emptied the ashes from the bottom of the fire.

This was the first day of our holiday in Cork. We were staying with my mum's cousin, Jim, and his wife, Sarah. They live in an enormous Victorian house on Eastern Road which is shared with students in winter and holiday-makers in summer. June was an in-between month, so there was plenty of space for mum and myself.

My mum had lost touch with most of her Irish relations because of an argument with her mother. Then, four years ago, Jim and Sarah contacted my mum. They wanted somewhere to stay, close to London, on the way back from their honeymoon in France. It was the first I had known of my mum's Irish relations. We never went to visit my mum's mother in Dagenham, so I didn't know any of the people Jim and Sarah talked about. It was strange to think that I lived so close to my mum's mother and yet Sarah and Jim knew far more about her than I did.

They had both seemed quite old to me to have just got married, although Sarah seemed far more interesting than most women of my mother's age. She had worked in Africa for ten years. 'Delivering babies in Kenya!' she used to say, as though she was joking.

Jim and Sarah had brought us to the novena service in the church. 'This is where Frank O'Connor made his famous "First Confession",' Jim whispered. It was the kind of whisper which made people ten benches away tune into Jim's conversation.

'Who's Frank O'Connor?' I asked my mum. She gave me her look of horror, normally reserved for my other questions like, 'Where does the Pope live?' or 'Do we really have to go to Mass on Sundays?'

'He's a very famous Irish writer.' She was still hissing. It would have been better if she whispered like Jim.

'That's a matter of debate,' Sarah interrupted.

'How do you mean?' my mother questioned Sarah in a gentler tone.

'I'll tell you later.'

The service was about to begin. It seemed as though everybody in Cork City had come to the novena, the nine days' prayer. Sarah said it was a tradition – like an annual carnival to celebrate a saint's day.

The bell rang to warn the congregation, who, as if carefully trained, stood up as one unit. Candles were placed all around the church, over the altar and in the different chapels. In a funny sort of way they made me feel more relaxed. It seemed strange to see those sorts of light in June – it was more like Christmas.

During the service my mother wept quietly into a number of disposable hankies. What's the point of coming, I thought to myself, if it upsets you this much? I wasn't upset. I thought of Dixon and Dunny sweating away back at school, aiming shots at goal and answering Murphy back when he told them not to wear trainers or white socks.

Why did Murphy have such a thing about white socks? His obsession infected people, so that even on Saturdays I would wander through the town square counting how many lads were wearing white socks. As the altar servers walked around to have the thurible topped up with incense, I strained to look at which of them was wearing white socks and wondered what Murphy would say if he was here.

At the end of the service the church emptied very slowly, as people placed their prayers, written on small bits of paper, into a box sitting before the altar.

'What did you pray for?' Sarah asked, as my mother walked up to place her written request in the box.

'For peace,' I lied. I'd thought about all sorts of things – my dad, my mates at school, my flaming English assignment – but I couldn't honestly say that I'd been praying. It didn't work anyway.

'You're such a lovely boy!' Sarah wrapped her arm around my shoulders and gazed at me as if I'd just given her an ice-cream with chocolate sauce. 'I prayed for a baby. I've brought that many babies into the world and yet me and Jim can't seem to have our own.'

Wasn't life complicated? My mum and dad didn't really appreciate me and they didn't live together any more, yet they had everything Sarah and Jim wanted.

Jim and Sarah walked up to the box with their request. I don't believe in magic, so I didn't write down, 'Please make my dad come back to our house.' If I didn't ask for things, I'd never be disappointed.

The car journey to Clonakilty, West Cork, seemed endless. All the way there Sarah played Irish songs on her car stereo. Every now and again as Christy Moore or Finbar Furey sang something slightly controversial, my mother would whoop or throw her head back and laugh. It was embarrassing.

Mum and I hired two bikes from a shop on the main street. The bike man recognized my mum as soon as she walked in. He shook her hand vigorously and said, 'You're very welcome, welcome home,' about five times. Then he turned to me. 'Is this your boy? Didn't he grow into a fine young man!' He shook hands, once again with vigour.

'Isn't it grand that you still come back? Aren't you a great woman now. God be with those days when you used to come with your mother and all the family, all those years ago.' As he spoke my mother laughed, and blushed slightly.

'It's different since my granny died, but I still like to come back and keep in touch. Anyway, Patrick and I just wanted a little break.'

'Well, good on you! What about himself, is he not over?' The bike man looked all around as if my dad might be hiding. He looked past Sarah, who seemed to be enjoying the reunion from a distance.

'No . . .' My mum faltered and then she put her hand on my arm, partly for support and partly as if to silence me. 'No, he's far too busy at work.' I looked at the gleaming mountain bikes, waiting for collection, hoping that my mum wouldn't tell this stranger what had happened.

'What at Ford's? Well, Jeez, aren't they the slave-drivers! They were the same when they were up here in Cork City.'

'No, he's not at Ford's any more. He's changed jobs. Well, he was made redundant a few years ago, so he retrained as a youth worker.' My mother's speech was well rehearsed. In Cork, people always assumed that my dad worked at Ford's just because we lived near Dagenham.

'Well, fair play to him, if it gets him off the factory floor. Now then, I suppose you want a couple of bikes for the day. Let me see for a minute what I can do for ye.'

The bikes were soon organized. Sarah went off to see some friends. Mum and I headed out to Inchy-doney.

I'd often heard how Mum had spent many happy childhood days on Inchydoney beach. 'In the summer you'd always see somebody you knew from

Dagenham,' my mother laughed, as she reminisced on her childhood days. 'It's different now. Only grannies live in Dagenham and they don't venture much further than Clacton for their seaside holiday.'

'What do you mean, only grannies live in Dagenham?' Sometimes I just didn't have a clue what my mum was on about.

'Do you realize, Patrick, on Christmas Day there's no one left in Dagenham. All the grannies have gone to Billericay or Harlow or Upminster for the day. You could hang your washing out across the street in Dagenham on Christmas Day and no one would pinch it because there's no one there.'

'What about the grandads?' I shouted, as she suddenly cycled ahead of me.

'They're all dead!'

As we cycled further along the side of the river estuary out towards the sea, I wanted to say, 'What about my dad? Where will he go for Christmas Day?' But I didn't want to push my luck.

We locked our bikes to a drainpipe on the side of the Inchydoney Hotel and sat on top of a cliff overlooking the Atlantic Ocean. There was very little activity in the sea – no small yachts sailing out towards the horizon or windsurfers and jet-skiers crashing on to the beach. It seemed strange. At Southend the sea was always busy. Here the sea was calm and undisturbed by any human life.

Looking towards the beach there were family groups sitting and playing together. Proper family groups. Mums, dads and children. Then the strangest feeling hit me – a sort of loneliness, and I so wished there was just one other person with us. It could be so difficult with my mum at times. Like now, when she just sat, looking beyond the beach and the cliffs out towards the sea, not talking, just looking. She could have just as easily been in our sitting-room looking out at the privet hedge.

If only Dixon or Dunny were here, we could have a kick-about on the beach or a splash-about in the water.

I didn't want to seem ungrateful, but it was a bit daft a thirteen-year-old boy going on holiday with his middle-aged mother. She's thirty-four, she still likes the Rolling Stones, she doesn't know the colour of Arsenal's home kit and she wonders why I spend so much time playing on my computer when I'm at home.

Then, as if I'd put a note in that box in church, this lad came up and said, 'How are ye?' and held his hand out.

'Fine, thanks.' I shook his hand and stood up. He was wearing a Celtic top and carrying a white leather football. When he smiled it looked as though his two front teeth were missing.

'We're short of a man. Will you come on our team?' His words brought a huge smile to my mother's face. She looked beyond us and waved at a woman standing near the beach who seemed to be watching the boy in the Celtic top. It must have been the boy's mother, scouring the beach and the cliff for an 'extra man'.

I followed the boy, Peadar down on to the beach, and, even though they put me in goal, I forgot about Dad, Mum, grannies, Dagenham and everything – even if it was just for a few hours.

9

MY FAMILY'S STORY

Cork City
Ireland

27 June

Dear Sister Mary Rita

Hope this letter finds you well. We're enjoying a lovely few days in Cork, and as Patrick is busy with his relations I thought I'd drop you a quick line.

I don't know if you remember that a few weeks ago I spoke to you briefly at a parents' evening and you remarked that there had been a big change in Patrick's attitude. I suggested that it was just adolescence. Well, I have to be honest with you because I'm so concerned about Patrick.

Patrick's father and I separated a few months ago. At first Patrick didn't seem to notice, so we didn't have to mention the subject. Then he started asking questions like, 'Why isn't Dad coming home after work?' and 'Why doesn't Dad live here any more?' I tried to answer as honestly as I could, but it was so difficult. I don't want to say much because I know I'll sound bitter. It wouldn't be right for Patrick to think badly about his father.

Most of the trouble started when Patrick had to write his life story for English. He had to find out a lot of information about his parents and grandparents. Patrick didn't complete his assignment because he was unable to glean any information from either Sean (his father) or myself. I just find it really difficult to talk about the early years of my marriage at the moment.

The reason I'm writing is this: first of all, Patrick desperately needs to talk to somebody. I have heard that you have been trained in working with troubled children, so would it be possible for you to talk to Patrick? It would be a great weight off my mind if I thought that he was talking to somebody who could encourage him to do his schoolwork. Secondly, do you know of any groups of people who are in a similar situation to myself - especially other women? If you're a Catholic and your marriage ends, you can be made to feel a terrible failure.

I hope that you don't mind me asking you these things. If Patrick isn't sorted out, he will probably end up with no qualifications and few prospects.

Thanks, in anticipation, for your help.

Kate Connolly

Jim and Sarah's
Cork

Thursday

Dear Sean

Just a quick note. Patrick is upstairs working, at long last, on his English assignment. Jim and Sarah have been able to tell him a good bit about his Cork ancestors. Sarah has really taken to him.

I just wanted to say thanks for taking us to Euston for the boat-train. It was kind of you. We'll be back in Essex on Sunday night. No doubt Patrick will want to see you fairly soon, so could you ring early next week to arrange something. He's been a bit quiet at times, but I imagine he's having a good old think about all sorts of things.

When we were at the seaside yesterday, he was invited to join in a football game on the beach. It came at just the right time - I think he was getting tired of my company.

Whatever happens, we must never stop talking about our son. He comes first.

Regards

Kate

Sarah's husband, Jim, spent twenty years working in London – on the roads and the buildings. People used to tell him how historical London was, but Jim thought it was a strange type of history – it was a history of royalty and people with money. Not ordinary people's history.

'Things are very different in Cork, Patrick . . .' Jim seemed to be confiding in me. 'It's more of a working people's city. I'm dead proud of it . . . but I suppose even Londoners are proud of their home town!'

As we looked out over the city of Cork from the top of St Patrick's Hill, my mum said, 'Cork seems to me to be more beautiful than Dublin.'

'You wouldn't want to be saying that to a Dubliner, Kate!' Jim laughed loudly at my mum's comments.

Jim told us all about how Cork was affected by the famine and the war of independence. I'd heard a little about the famine in history at school – but it seemed so long ago. I never thought of it affecting relations of mine. He pointed out the Shandon Church and all the other important landmarks. I wanted to see where my grandma had been born. Even though I didn't know her I was curious to know where she had grown up. Mum wanted to go to Harrington Square, where Frank O'Connor had lived for a while.

'You won't find any Irish people looking for Harrington Square,' Sarah said. 'It's all Germans and Americans. The Irish aren't a bit interested.'

'Why is that?' my mother asked with some concern.

'Well . . . a mixture of things. Many of O'Connor's neighbours recognized themselves in his work and they were insulted by how he portrayed them. They felt he was anti-Irish.'

As I listened to them talking about Ireland and Irish writers I felt confused. It was the same sort of feeling I had when my mum and dad tried to explain what was happening to our family.

I wanted to ask questions, but I never knew what to ask. They all knew so much. I didn't know which questions to ask. I wanted to know all about my mum's family – but at the same time I didn't want to appear too . . . nosy. That's why I never knew where to start.

As we walked along, Sarah told me about my mum's parents. My mum and Jim walked ahead, out of earshot. Sarah seemed to anticipate my questions and she told me about the bits of my family's Cork that I really wanted to know – where my grandparents were born, where they grew up and why they came to England.

My Life Story

PART ONE

My grandmother, that is, my mother's mother, was born and brought up in a small house in Cork City in Ireland. Her family lived near the Youghal Old Road, which sort of runs along the top of the city. They lived close to the Collins Barracks, one of the oldest barracks in the British Isles.

When my grandmother was young she used to wait around close to the old women who sat outside their doors during the summer months and listen to their stories. She always knew when they were discussing something scandalous as they would say, 'Hush, now, the child is listening.' Most of the time, though, she had to help her mother with the housework. In those days women had very hard lives.

My grandfather lived two streets away from my grandmother. They knew one another when they were growing up, but they didn't really like each other. Many years later, they met in Essex and married.

After the war there was a serious unemployment problem in Cork, so many of the young people had to leave their homes to find work in England or America. My grandfather went to work in England – in Dagenham, actually. He worked at Ford's. There were so many people from Cork working there that they used to say, 'Cork City, County Dagenham'. Although it felt strange for my grandfather being away from home, it helped having so many of his friends around him.

My grandmother was a waitress in different places in London. One weekend she went to stay with an old friend and her husband in Dagenham. That's when she met my grandfather. My mother tells me that her father was not at all romantic. He proposed to my grandmother by saying that it would be cheaper to pay just one lot of rent. In those days, that was a proposal of marriage.

My mother was born at Rush Green Hospital a year after my grandparents married. She was born in 1957. She was followed by two sisters – Bridget and Anne. My two aunties have both emigrated. Bridget is in Canada, Anne is in Australia. When they were leaving home my grandmother was very sad. She thought that when she left her homeland it would mean that her own children would be able to live close to her. My mother said that the children of emigrants don't know where they really belong, so they wander a great deal themselves.

END OF PART ONE

Early on Friday evening we wandered through the shopping area. A boy, about my age, stood on a street corner selling 'Free Nelson Mandela' T-shirts from a big cardboard box.

'You'll have a job selling those, son,' Jim advised the T-shirt seller.

'Why?' As he spoke, the boy continued to search the street and the crowd for any signs of the Garda.

'He's free!' Jim pointed at the T-shirts.

'Who?' The boy now looked straight at Jim.

'Mandela. He's free. He was released the other year. Jim picked up the T-shirt and held it close to the street seller's face.

'Was he? Well, good luck to him. Anyways – Ireland were knocked out of the World Cup the other year, but I'm still selling "Republic of Ireland – Italia 1990" T-shirts.' He continued to look straight at Jim, though now a little more menacingly.

'Well, son . . .' Jim hesitated. For once he was stuck for words. 'Fair play to you. You're a real salesman.'

We wandered around the centre of Cork looking for traditional music. It was our last night, and Mum wanted to go back with good memories.

A woman lay across the pavement. She looked as though she was dead. My mother muttered, 'Disgusting!' and walked around her. People sought for interesting window displays, posters, clouds, anything to divert their attention, their eyes, away from the dead woman. I wondered why no one would take her away and bury her.

Then two Italian men bent down and asked her if she was all right. She raised her head slightly and said, 'No.' People continued to walk over her, around her – some gathered beside her now the responsibility had been taken from them. There was a lot of tutting.

The Italians lifted her to the side of the pavement and leaned her against a shop window. She wasn't dead, just drunk. Even so, only these two foreigners would care for her. It made me feel so sad.

Later that evening we saw her wander into the main road and flag down a passing BMW. 'Take me home,' she shouted at the driver and then collapsed on to his bonnet. Risen from the dead, she was making her mark, once again, on the world.

She was about the same age as my gran, my dad's mum. I wondered where this woman's children and grandchildren were. And if her grandson had to write his life story, what would he say about her, his grandmother?

I thought about my life story again. I was pleased with what I'd written and it felt as though there was a great weight off my mind. I already knew about my dad's family, so I'd be able to write that chapter back home. Writing all about my mum's family had really got me started. I was thankful for Sarah. She was very understanding and she'd really helped me a lot.

Sooner or later I had to write about my parents – one of them would have to answer my questions. That was the first thing that I was going to do when I got back home. Ask them those questions.

Where did you meet? Where did you get married? What was I like when I was little? Tell me something funny about when I was a baby. Why did you split up? Why don't you live together any more? Tell me. Tell me the truth.

10
THE JOURNEY HOME

It was very late on Sunday evening when we walked into the living-room. In a voice full of tiredness from travelling, Mum said, 'Don't worry about school in the morning, Patrick. I'll ring Mr Murphy later on – tell him the boat was delayed.'

It hadn't been delayed. We visited more of mum's cousins in Dublin and they persuaded us to change our sailing. Then the trains weren't running out of Fenchurch Street because of engineering works, so we had to catch a bus to Barking. The whole journey home was a bit like a nightmare. On the train from Holyhead to Euston the only spare seats were next to a couple whose baby screamed all the way through Wales and the Midlands. Just as we passed through Nuneaton it began to stop.

On top of all that my mother was telling this couple all about my first months. 'Aren't the first few days of a child's life fascinating? That's if you're not too daunted by becoming a parent for the first time.' The couple smiled and nodded. They nodded almost all the time as they rocked their screaming bundle. It seemed as though my mother was talking to herself. 'Do you know what I thought was absolutely incredible?' Pause. Mum waited for a response, a little 'What?', but they just nodded. Still, she continued. 'The way my baby sort of unfolded in his first days. When he was born he was all sort of . . . squashed up and tucked in. Then, day by day, his nose and his ears unfolded and opened out. Like a little flower blossoming.'

'Mum . . . be quiet,' I whispered. This was so embarrassing. All I needed now was for Dixon and Dunny to sit near by and overhear my mother. As it was, an old lady sat across the aisle. She smiled, as if in absolute delight, at my mum's words. She was reading *Woman's Weekly* and wearing a woollen hat, probably one knitted from a pattern in her magazine. The whole carriage knew more about me as a baby than I did.

'Can I ring Dad when I get in?' I asked really nicely, but Mum looked hurt. I had brought her back to reality and, at the same time, announced to our travelling friends our domestic situation.

'Provided it's not too late. We don't want to disturb his work.' My mother was pretending that there were still roses growing around our cottage door. Well, we didn't even live in a cottage, we lived in a 'terraced townhouse'. The old lady with the woollen hat and the *Woman's Weekly* smiled at us. It was a sad sort of smile. She wasn't daft.

Walking into the living-room it all hit me – Mum, Dad, school, my life story. There was so much to be sorted out and my head ached from the screaming bundle and the noisy double-decker bus that struggled over every flyover on the A13. I wished I was glad to be home, but I wasn't. I wished I felt happy to be back, but I didn't. Still, at least tomorrow was Monday and – oh, bliss – Mum said I didn't have to go to school.

Dagenham

Sunday evening

Kate

I'll be away on a course until Wednesday. Please tell Patrick - he said he would contact me as soon as he returned.

Sorry for the short notice - it's just unavoidable. Somebody dropped out and we have to have a representative from this unit present on the course. It's about the changes in the law which come into force fairly soon.

Hopefully I'll be able to meet up with Pat on Saturday.

Must shoot

Sean

Holy Family Convent
Timberfoot Place
Langdon Newtown
Essex

1 July

Dear Kate

First of all, may I express my sympathy for your personal sadness at this time. Be assured of my thoughts and prayers. Marriage breakdown has become such a common thing in Western Europe, and in this area in particular. It brings so much unhappiness, not only for the married partners, but also for their children.

Patrick, as you mention in your letter, is coping in his own way. He is grieving for the death of his parents' marriage. We must all try to understand this. He may pass through this fairly quickly or it may take him some time. It may be something he carries with him into adult life. It is up to those who care about him to ensure that he doesn't become cynical about adult relationships. I will remember Patrick (and his father) in my prayers too.

I have heard of an organization within the Church called 'Keeping the Faith' or 'KTF'. They are a group of people who have been deserted by their marriage partners and, as a consequence, they are separated or divorced. They are called

'Keeping the Faith' because they recognize the fact that the Church does not allow them to remarry and they want to remain faithful to that teaching, that law. Therefore, KTF is not a place to meet other partners, it's a support group. Each session begins with a recitation of the rosary, so it's very spiritual. Their patron is Mary, because in many ways she was a single parent (although she wasn't separated or divorced).

If you are interested in joining KTF just let me know and I will find out the contact address and telephone number.

Hopefully Patrick will feel renewed and refreshed after his short break. I'll try to engineer an opportunity to speak to him. I feel that he's rather reluctant to accept a listening ear at present. However, I will endeavour to do my best if you feel it will help.

If I can be of any more assistance, please do not hesitate to contact me – either at school or at the convent.

Yours in prayer

Rita Keane

Rita Keane
(Sister Mary Rita)

My Life Story

PART TWO

My father's parents are from the west of Ireland. My gran is from Mayo and my grandad is from County Galway – from Connemara. He grew up in a small town called Spiddal, which overlooks the Atlantic Ocean. My grandad says that Connemara is a fashionable place now because it is so wild and rugged. Many people visit this part of Ireland because of its outstanding natural beauty. Grandad says that people don't look beyond the beauty of the landscape – they don't see that if somewhere is wild and rugged it's almost impossible for those who live there to make a living from the land. This sometimes makes him very angry.

When he was twenty my grandad left Spiddal. He didn't understand at the time, but he says, looking back on things, he must have been heartbroken. It is hard for my grandad to admit this. Normally he only gets upset when his horse loses – he is mad on horse-racing.

When my grandma was growing up she wanted to be a farmer. In those days girls were only encouraged to do women's jobs. There weren't many jobs around Mayo, so she moved to England. Now she has the best vegetable garden on her estate in Dagenham. She has won the Vic Feather

Memorial Cup five times, for the neatness of her garden and the quality of her vegetables. My gran says that the soil is as good as the soil in Mayo, but the air is not as sweet. My grandparents had three children – the eldest of whom was my father, Sean. After him came Marian and Teresa.

My father used to work at Ford's, training apprentices, but after he was made redundant he retrained at a college in London. Now we don't see much of him, as he's a very busy youth and community worker.

END OF PART TWO

11
SOMETHING'S WRONG

I knocked gently on Murphy's door (so that he might think it was a girl), whilst clutching the first two parts of my life story. My mother had persuaded me to present it in a clear plastic folder, so that it looked better. I told her that nothing like that impressed Murphy. Normally he shouts 'Enter', but this morning he came to the door and just opened it slightly.

'Oh . . . D. P. Connolly. How pleased I am to see you!' He spoke in such a sweet voice that I knew he didn't mean it. Then, 'Where were you yesterday? I believe you arrived back from holiday two days ago.' This was more like the Murphy I knew. Harsh, unkind, cruel.

'My mum rang you.'

'That's a funny name for a place. Was the weather good there?' Murphy began to speak in the sugar-sweet tone again. Honest, I think teachers take a Master's Degree in sarcasm.

'Sorry, sir, I was at home yesterday. We arrived back late on Sunday. My mum said she was going to ring you.'

'Well, she didn't.' The old Murphy again. 'So, as far as I'm concerned, you were truanting.'

'If you want to ring her at work, sir, she'll tell you the truth. I honestly wasn't truanting.' This was hard to believe.

I tried to be as quiet and polite as I could, but it felt as though Murphy was prodding me in the chest, wanting me to respond violently, teasing me and taunting me until I did something really wrong, like spit in his face. I couldn't be bothered.

'Do you think that I've got nothing better to do than ring your mother and check out whether or not you're telling the truth?'

'Yes, sir.' I spoke quietly and I tried to keep all my face muscles still. Sometimes I broke into a nervous smile involuntarily (and without any control, as Dunny would say). That didn't help.

'What do you mean, "Yes, sir"?' This was Murphy at his confusing best. It was getting to be like one of those meaningless conversations out of a television situation comedy.

'Yes, sir, you have got better things to do.'

I could tell by the slight change in Murphy's expression that I'd outpaced him. He'd lost the thread of the conflict. He was about to change the subject – perhaps to say something about my tie or shirt. There was a little embroidered patch on the pocket. He'd notice it and tell me that it wasn't school uniform. As it was, I stepped in first.

'Here's the first two parts of my life story, sir.'

'What a surprise. D. P. Connolly has actually done some work.' Murphy took the work from me and looked at the first page. 'I hope that this is all your own work, Connolly.' He eyed me suspiciously.

'My family did help me with the research, sir.'

He didn't say anything else. The telephone was ringing. He took the work from me and with his free hand he waved me away. I have noticed people wave at annoying flying insects in a similar manner.

The Year Elevens had left, so the best pitches were available to us at dinner-times. The weather had changed – it was a lot warmer – so our kick-abouts didn't last for the whole of the hour. We'd lie down and talk without looking at one another. It's much easier to say what you really mean when you're like that.

We talked about our option choices and what we wanted to do when we left school. I wanted to work in a garden centre. Dunny said that was a job for 'thickos'. Dixon wanted to work in an old people's home – doing drama with the geriatrics. Me and Dunny laughed so much. But Dixon wasn't joking. We laughed until it hurt and then Dixon stormed off in a mood. He walked a few metres away and sat with his back to us, plucking great chunks of grass from the ground and then flinging them away. Some of the girls sat down beside Dixon. They all loved him and he was so natural with them. He didn't treat them as different or special. I envied him.

He said all the right things in class discussions, things like, 'There should be far more women in Parliament' and 'Why aren't girls in this school allowed to wear trousers in winter?' And the thing was, he didn't do it to curry favour with the girls. He sincerely believed those things. The girls knew that and they loved him. Not just because he was attractive or because he was funny, but because he was gentle and honest.

Dunny and I watched from a distance as Dixon went up another ten steps in the girls' estimation as he told them of his wish. To work in an old people's home.

HOLY FAMILY SCHOOL · LANGDON · ESSEX

Mr & Mrs S. Connolly
24 Lansbury Gardens
Langdon
Essex

28 June

Dear Parents

During the next few weeks your daughter/son **Darren** will be involved in making subject option choices. You are invited to a meeting in school on **Thursday 4 July** at **8 p.m.** to discuss your child's option choices. These choices will shape the final two years of your child's education in this school. You are encouraged to attend.

We look forward to meeting you then.

Yours faithfully

M. Brodie-Vasquez

Ms M. Brodie-Vasquez, M.Ed.
Careers Counsellor and Head of Year

Lansbury Gardens

Tuesday

Dear Sean

Thanks for your note. We arrived home on Sunday evening after a lovely short break. Patrick was worried about where you were yesterday, so it's a relief for him to know.

This is just a quick note written in great haste on my way out to work. There's a meeting at the school on Thursday at 8 p.m. to discuss Patrick's option choices for the next two years. I think it's a specific appointment to see the Careers Teacher. Will you be able to make it? I'm sure Patrick would be very pleased if you could be there.

After the meeting, would you like to go out for a drink somewhere? I've been thinking a great deal these last few days and I need to talk to you. I mean *talk*, not shout, I promise.

See you Thursday.

Best wishes

Kate

As soon as I walked into the house I knew something was wrong. Everywhere was quiet. I had this strange feeling. If I'm honest, I think the feeling had been there all day. Like the sort of headache you experience when there's going to be a thunderstorm. You really wish for the storm to break so that your headache will go away – even though you might be frightened of storms.

The first thing was, Gran was in the living-room. My gran had hardly visited us since my dad left. I suppose there wasn't much reason for her to visit now that her son was no longer here. She was dusting the furniture. Very slowly she moved the duster along the backs of the chairs and the table legs. I watched, transfixed and terrified. Maybe my mum and dad had been killed and now I was an orphan. I'd come home every evening to Gran dusting. No, that hadn't happened because I'd thought it. If you think it, then it doesn't happen.

'How are ye, Patrick?' she spoke so quietly.

'What's up, Gran? What are you doing here?'

My mother's bedroom was filled with a strange smell – sort of sweet and perfumed, yet sickly. My mum lay on the bed, covered with her duvet, although she was still wearing her working clothes. For a moment I thought of the woman in Cork, the one who lay stretched across the street before running in front of BMWs.

'I'm sorry, Pat,' Mum whispered. It seemed to be

a real struggle for her. 'I'm sorry, Pat . . .' Then, 'Is your gran still here?'

'Yes. What's up, Mum?' What was she so sorry about? It crossed my mind that whilst she was in such a receptive and apologetic mood I'd ask her about the Russian exchange with our school next year.

'Ask your gran. She'll tell you.' Her head fell to one side and she closed her eyes. In old films the leading lady did this just before she died, but I knew my mum was all right; she started snoring almost straight away.

Gran had finished the dusting and sat on the arm of one of the chairs watching an Australian series. It was one of those embarrassing bits where the young attractive couple are locked in one another's arms. Her eyes twinkle with joy and a sort of sadness as she says, 'What about your wife?' He looks beyond her, probably at the script written in big letters, and says, 'My wife doesn't understand me.'

I was relieved when Gran switched it off and shouted, 'That old Aussie rubbish. Do you know, Patrick, that's pure rubbish. I think that puts ideas into people's heads!'

I watched the dot disappear from the screen and thought about how it disappeared more quickly recently. I didn't know what was going on and nobody was telling me. My gran had been dusting our living-room whilst my mother was lying in her bed, fully dressed, smelling of some sort of alcohol. I didn't even know if my dad was alive or dead.

'Do you like liver and onions, Patrick?' This was just typical of grown-ups – I thought my gran would have known better. I arrive home from school, there's a sinister atmosphere in the house, the grown-ups are clinging on to all the information, yet again, and my gran wants to know if I like liver and onions. My gran would probably make cups of tea for people who'd been involved in a bad road accident. 'I think my leg's come off . . .' 'Oh, don't worry about that! Would you like a cup of tea whilst you're waiting for the ambulance?'

'No thanks Gran, I don't feel all that hungry.'

'Are you sickening for something?' She lifted my head to look into my eyes. Gran said as far as truth and health were concerned, eyes were the big give-away.

'I felt fine until I came in, Gran. I've just got this funny feeling in my stomach. What are you doing here, Gran?' She took a deep breath and looked away from me.

'Your mum . . . Kate . . . asked me to come over.'

'Why? What's up? What's been going on?' I sat on the edge of the chair – the wooden bit where the cushion finishes.

'She's had a bit of bad news and she couldn't cope by herself so . . . I offered . . .' Her voice trailed off.

'What bad news?' I was annoyed with Gran drawing things out and not finishing anything properly. 'Is it Dad?'

'Yes, it's about your dad.'

'What's wrong, Gran?' The thunder exploded in my head and the panic filled my throat. I felt as though I couldn't swallow.

'He's not dead or anything, Pat. He isn't injured and he hasn't been in an accident, so calm down. Now, I can't say much, but it's to do with your mum and dad.'

He's not dead, he's not injured, he hasn't been in an accident. There couldn't be anything else to worry about, could there? It's so difficult when grown-ups don't tell you the full story.

Even though my head was pounding, I started to write the next bit of my life story – all about my mum's schooldays. On the boat back from Ireland she tried to tell me stories about her childhood to keep my mind off my overturning stomach – it was a rough crossing.

I still didn't know the full story.

My Life Story

PART THREE

My mother went to an all-girls convent school at the age of eleven. Her parents were really proud of her as it was a grammar school – she had passed her eleven-plus examination. They were especially proud of her the first time they saw her wearing her school uniform. As they weren't very well off it was a struggle for them to buy all the uniform and equipment, but they considered that it was worth it. My mother worked hard at school although she used to play some practical jokes on the nuns.

Once a month, on Sundays, the nuns used to have a 'Come and See' afternoon. My mum had heard from some of the older girls that the nuns used to serve the most delicious cakes at these events, so Mum and her best friend, Carole, used to go along quite often.

When they had been to about four 'Come and See' afternoons, Sister Mary Benigna thought that my mum had a vocation. (My mum says that they didn't think Carole had a vocation because she wasn't clever enough.) Carole and my mum only went because of the cakes and because they liked the beautiful singing at Mass. Sister Mary Benigna contacted my grandparents and invited them to a

'Come and See' afternoon. My mother was horrified, because she knew that her parents would think it a good thing if she became a nun. They said that she wouldn't have to worry about bills or food, she'd always have a job, and one day she'd probably be a headmistress. By this time my mother had discovered boys, flared jeans and Deep Purple. She thought they were even more attractive than beautiful singing and delicious cakes.

My mum says that some days she wishes she did have a vocation all those years ago. She thinks that life would have been a lot simpler and easier to cope wIth.

END OF PART THREE

12
THE FANCY WOMAN

Gran made the liver and onions anyway. It was a warm evening – sort of egg-salad weather – but that didn't deter my gran. 'We all need iron at this moment in time,' she said gravely, placing the dinner in front of me. Then she sat in front of the television and looked at the pictures accompanying the news. The volume was turned down. She kept looking to see how I was progressing with the liver. When there was just a little left on my plate she looked intently at the news and said, in a flat, unemotional voice, 'Your father has moved out.'

Is that all? I thought to myself. I was so relieved. Gran was upset because my dad, her son, had moved out, left home again. I half smiled – mainly with a warm feeling of relief, but it was mixed with a tint of apprehension. If that was all, what was all the fuss about? I was a bit annoyed with my dad because he hadn't told me he was moving. I knew things were hectic and that he was on a course this week, but he could have told me that he was thinking about it.

'Why has he moved out, Gran?' Her face was knotted and angry. She took deep breaths and looked at some royal opening of a new road.

'I don't think his old Irish parents are good enough for him any more.' Gran's words stung me. What did she mean?

‘What do you mean, Gran?’ I wished she’d look at me. I stared into a space between Gran and the television and asked her again. ‘What do you mean? I don’t understand.’

‘He’s moved in with a woman. His fancy woman. In Forest Gate. She has a house in Forest Gate.’

She spoke it as though it was a list. I’ll tell you why Patrick:

1. He’s moving out.
2. He’s moved in with a woman.
3. She has a house in Forest Gate.
4. She is his fancy woman.

I’d never heard the expression ‘Fancy Woman’ before. I thought of her like a Spanish flamenco dancer, wearing a red bolero top and a matching long skirt, full of frills. In my mind she smiled broadly and wore flowers in her long, dark hair. She was so gaudy. I hated her already. ‘His fancy woman.’ Gran had spat the words at me as if it was partly my fault. It was nothing to do with me.

‘God love your poor mother.’ She spoke gently now. Then suddenly, impatiently, ‘Arra, she was too good for him. I always said that. God love her. Hadn’t she prayed for a reconciliation at the novena in Cork. She came home full of good intentions, things were going to be great again. Then . . . your man takes off with some fancy piece. God love your poor mother . . .’ She folded her hands again and again. Then she cried. Silent tears running down her face, across her lined features. Some fell off her face and on to her ‘Cead Mile Failte’ apron.

A horrible grey cloud forced its way into the room, filling up all the corners, muffling the words my gran spoke, stopping the air from reaching my lungs, knocking my head from side to side. If someone had died I would have felt better. All I could think was, 'Why didn't my dad, *my dad*, tell me?'

I opened the window, the room seemed so stuffy. People rushed along the street on their way home from the City. They were rushing home to normality. How I wished my mum was just rushing home. How I wished that it was just a normal July day.

Everyone can see the trains passing through Langdon. In the winter evenings they look like luminous snakes slipping between the houses and the shopping centre. In the summer the brightly clad workers pour out of the carriages, all sweaty and crumpled. Once I saw a programme on television about South African workers returning to their townships at night; it reminded me of Langdon. As one unit, Langdon streams into London every day. When it's ten o'clock in the morning, Langdon is out at work in the City.

About four years ago my mum went back to work. She couldn't get a decent job around here, so she waited until I went to secondary school and then started travelling into the City every day. She works for an insurance company. My dad and mum used to have arguments about her working in the City. Dad was always giving out about capitalism. I wondered if his woman in the flamenco outfit was a capitalist.

It felt better with the windows open. I made a cup of tea for my mum. Gran seemed sort of paralysed. She was slumped in the chair, not wanting to talk. It was so unlike her; she always had something to say. Her angry words kept hitting my brain every few minutes. 'Your dad has a fancy woman.' I kept wondering about how this would affect our Saturdays. Even more importantly, how would I fit it into my life story? Some people in my class had stepfathers and stepmothers, but I'd never heard any of them say that their dads had 'fancy' women.

Mum was sitting up, dressed in an old track suit, when I gave her the tea. 'Has your gran told you?'

I wanted to pretend that I didn't know, so that I could hear another version of the story, but I just said, 'Yes.' I didn't know what to say to my mum. I didn't understand why they weren't living together anyway. They had tried explaining, but I just didn't get it. Now there was this. Mum stroked my hair as if I was the one who was ill.

'I went drinking at dinner-time, Patrick.'

'Did you?' What was I supposed to say?

'Do you know how your dad told me? Do you? Did your gran tell you?' Her speech was still a bit shaky.

'No.' I spoke quietly. I didn't really want to know how my dad told her. Just knowing it was bad enough.

'He rang your gran from his "course" and asked her to ring me at work. Can you believe that? That's your father for you!'

'Sorry, Mum.' That's all I could think of.

'So . . . you know what I did? I pretended it was my birthday, went out with a friend and got smashed! Smashed! What a way for a mother to behave!'

She looked furiously towards the window. Why was nobody looking at me? What had I done wrong?

Grandad came at half-eight. He knocked softly at the back door and walked in quietly, just as if somebody had died. He didn't say anything much. He didn't even ask me about school. 'How's herself?' he asked my gran.

'Not too bad, now. She's getting over the shock. Patrick has been very kind.' Gran stroked my head as she spoke.

'We'll go then.'

'Fine.'

'Behave yourself, Patrick. Don't let your mother down; she has enough to contend with at the moment.' This was my gran's awkward goodbye.

Grandad ruffled my hair and they left, closing the kitchen door softly behind them.

I thought about those photographs in the loft. It looked as though we'd never take them down again.

24 Lansbury Gardens
Langdon
Essex

Wednesday

Dear Sister Mary Rita

We've all had a bit of a shock in the last twenty-four hours. Nobody has died or anything like that, but I can't bring myself to write about it just yet.

I wanted to write and warn you because I think Patrick will be in a very delicate state today. Would you please pass the message on to Mr Murphy. He's putting Patrick under a bit of pressure at the moment (rightly so, in my opinion), but I don't think he'll be able to take it today.

Thanks for your help.

Kate Connolly

PS I've told Patrick that this note is about a retreat, so please be careful what you say to him.

13

WHAT'S GOING ON?

The curtains in my bedroom are quite thin, so in summer the sun shines directly on to my face, nudging me awake at about half-past six.

Just as I was beginning to feel optimistic, I remembered – double Murphy. Two lessons of English. That's all I needed. I'd almost finished my life story, just one more chapter on how my parents met and then a bit about my early life. I might have to leave bits out.

Mum was in the kitchen, making my sandwiches, as if everything was normal. As if dad was going to come down the stairs, kiss her on the back of the head and say, 'What . . . no sausages?' as he used to every morning when he was in a good mood.

'Patrick, can you take this note in to Sister Mary Rita.' Mum pointed at a letter on the table. 'It's about a retreat I'm supposed to be going on.'

'Is Gran coming again?' I put the note in my blazer pocket as I asked.

'Yes, though God knows why.' She buttered the bread furiously. 'I think she feels guilty because it's her son. As if something she allowed him to do in his childhood has made him behave in this way. Yes . . . I think we'll be seeing quite a lot of Gran . . . the sins of the sons . . .'

Mum rambled on like that for a few minutes. She

wasn't really talking to me. At the moment she seemed to be either angry or crying. There was nothing in between. The holiday in Ireland, where she was so happy and relaxed, seemed a long time ago. We had only been back for two days. My dad was supposed to be on a course but he wasn't. Gran would be back, dusting and cooking liver and onions. I liked my gran, but she was better in Dagenham, better in her garden. On top of everything – double Murphy, and I still hadn't finished my life story.

Dixon and Dunny waited for me, as usual, at the top gates. We met there most mornings, then went over to the field for a kick-about. Dixon had passed through his 'drama with the geriatrics' phase, so he was talking to us again. I desperately wanted to tell them about my dad, but I didn't know how. I'd thought about it all the way to school, but I didn't know where to start. I thought about how I could bring the subject casually into the conversation.

'Hey, guess what . . .?'
'Do you want to hear the latest . . .?'
'I've had some bad news . . .'
'You won't believe this, but . . .'
'Hey, listen . . .'

Dunny told us a joke and I tried to laugh. He nudged me, as if I was half asleep, then said, 'What's up with you?'

'Yeah . . .' Dixon interrupted, before I could answer. 'What *is* up with you? You're acting a bit . . . funny this morning.' He made a sort of insane face and pushed me gently.

I kicked a crushed Pepsi can out of the way, laughed a bit more and said, 'Nothing.' There are no clichés or ready-made phrases to tell people about the things your mum and dad will do to your life.

'You don't want to let Murphy get to you, D. P. C.,' Dunny said, as if he'd discovered the reason for my quietness.

I handed the note into the staff-room. Murphy came to the door. 'Can I ask a very big favour?' he said, not waiting for my reply. 'We've got some visitors coming into our lesson today. Would you be prepared to read an extract from your life story?'

The visitors were from our German twin town. They sat at the front of the library, smiling, nodding their heads and examining every detail of the décor and furnishings. Murphy introduced them in his friendly *cappuccino* manner, talking about the importance of European links. He talked a bit about the variety of pupils in the school, in particular about our ethnic backgrounds. Xavier Fernandes read an extract from his life story first. It was about his parents leaving Tanzania and coming to England in the 1960s. His family were originally from Goa in southern India. Xavier had cousins in almost every year at school. They treated one another more like brothers and sisters.

Then it was my turn. Murphy introduced me: 'Now we're going to hear an extract from Darren's life story. The Irish are one of the largest ethnic groups in this area. Many of them came to Britain during the 1940s and 1950s, looking for work. They have stayed, helped to build Catholic schools, like this one, and strengthened the Church in this country. I know that many of our visitors have been to Ireland and I know, also, that you were very impressed with the music and culture there. Well, Darren will read a little about his background and maybe it will help you to understand more about the Irish in Britain.'

I walked to the front. For once, I felt proud of my Irish grandparents, just for the fact that they were Irish. It was a strange sort of feeling. I'd never heard Murphy speaking like this before. It was as if he was another person in front of visitors.

The German visitors smiled at me. One stood and shook my hand. Normally I'd be feeling really nervous by now, but the visitors had made me feel quite relaxed.

Things were going very well. Murphy had asked me to read the bit about my grandparents leaving Mayo and Connemara. My dad's parents. I had almost finished my bit; I was just reading, '. . . the eldest of which was my father, Sean,' when the words on the page disappeared. My mouth went dry as I tried to finish. I cleared my throat as best I could and looked back at the page. The words swam before me. I tried to focus on the word Sean, because I knew that was the last word I'd read. I couldn't find it. I could hear coughing. It was muffled as though I was inside a heavy curtain.

I looked intently at the page. What should I do? I

had finished in mid-sentence. People shuffled. I couldn't see a thing. I could feel the redness creeping up my neck and over my face. A guffaw was silenced – probably by a look from Murphy.

It seemed as though the whole world was standing there, looking at me making a fool of myself, waiting for somebody to burst the balloon, just so they could laugh and point at me. It felt as though years were passing. Still I couldn't find the words.

'Is that it? Have you finished, Darren?' Murphy spoke with a gentleness I had never heard before. It was so quiet. Or was it the thick curtain?

'No,' I replied. Then a tear escaped from my eye and landed on the missing words. 'No, I haven't finished . . . but I don't know what to do any more.'

I couldn't help it. The tears were rolling down my cheeks, on to my work. The shuffling stopped. The coughs were cured. There wasn't a sound – just my sniffling, as I searched for the tissue that didn't exist.

Mortified, I walked to the door as every eye in the world followed. I felt naked and cold. It shouldn't bother me. I don't know why I was so upset. I'm nearly fourteen and boys shouldn't cry – but I had this strange feeling. For the first time in my life I felt as though nobody loved me or even cared about me. It was like standing alone and cold in the middle of Antarctica, with the ice starting to melt under my feet.

Somebody opened the door as my sniffles became sobs. I didn't care who saw me. When you're this lonely, it doesn't really matter what people think about you.

I walked. Somebody held my arm. Another door opened. I could hear muffled voices – women clucking and worrying. I sat in a chair. The familiar posters sneered at me. 'A tea-break is God's apostrophe.' Then a voice said, 'Do you want to talk about it?'

'No!' I shouted it so all the school could hear. Especially those clucking outside the door. 'No!' This time it was a scream. My eyes began to focus again. It was our Head of Year. I could do without this.

'What's wrong, Darren?' She looked at me sympathetically. Deep down she was just nosy – they all were. It would make an interesting story at a dinner party: 'How I sorted out this really naughty boy.' All the guests would lean forward and listen intently, with their elbows on the table. They'd think how marvellous she is. Well, she isn't.

'Can I go home, please?' I had wanted it to sound polite but it didn't. It was as though I didn't have any control over the way my mouth was working.

'What's wrong, Darren?' she asked again.

'Nothing!' My shoulders shook. It was the middle of summer and I was cold.

'Do you want to talk about it?' Again and again. It hurt my head.

'No!'

'Are you sure?'

'Yes! Leave me alone!' I wanted to go.

'Darren!'

'Get lost! I want to go home.' With that I stood, knocking my chair over as I did, walked out of the room and straight out of school. My bag, with all my books, was in the library, along with the Germans.

My head cleared as I reached the end of the drive. I could hear again. A car drew up beside me – it was Sister Mary Rita.

'Do you want a lift home?' I did, but I didn't want to have to talk to anyone.

'Only if you're going that way, Sister.'

'Right, hop in.' She cleared a pile of books and papers from the front seat and just threw them behind. 'Anyway, I've got a letter for your mother. It's about a retreat she was going to go on. Will you give it to her?'

I took the letter and went to put it in my blazer. It was in the library, with the Germans. I hoped they wouldn't take it as a souvenir.

Leaning on the door, I looked out of the window. Sister Mary Rita didn't talk. She hummed and whistled along with a tune on her car radio.

Holy Family School
Newtown Road
Langdon

Wednesday

Dear Kate

Just a very quick note in reply to yours. Patrick, God love him, has been in a really bad way at school today. I think he's in a state of shock. Mr Murphy thinks he's had a type of panic attack. You might need to take him to the doctor.

If you need any help this evening, or if you just want somebody to talk to, do ring me at the convent.

Be assured of my prayers for you all at this difficult time. Patrick needs a lot of reassurance and love at the moment.

Must dash.

Rita Keane.

'Jesus, Mary and Joseph! You gave me the greatest shock. I honestly thought there were burglars in the house.' My gran was white with fear as she shouted at me. If my head didn't ache so much it would have been funny. Gran was so nervous at times.

'What are you doing home? Are you ill? What's the matter?'

Questions, questions, questions. When Sister Mary Rita dropped me off outside the house she didn't ask anything. She just looked at me and said, very softly, 'I hope you're feeling better tomorrow, Patrick.' Sometimes, when people are gentle and kind, it can be almost as painful as when they're nasty. Sometimes, nastiness is easier to cope with.

Dixon and Dunny, in fact all my class, had been in that room where I'd made such a fool of myself. I could never go back. They had seen my tears, my embarrassment. I'd shown them my pain. I could never walk into school with my head up. I'm almost fourteen; grown men don't cry.

Thinking about it made me cry again, in front of my gran. The questions were silenced. She moved towards me and gently touched my hand. 'God love you, Pat. It's always the youngsters who suffer.'

'What's going on?' I shouted it so loud that Gran stood back as if the words had physically struck her. 'Why did my dad leave? What's wrong with me?' I was screaming now. Gran moved right away and made the sign of the cross, like she does when there's lightning. 'Do you know what, Gran? I might as well be dead!' I spat the words out viciously. It was true. Nobody would miss me –

certainly not my dad. My mum only thought about herself, and I couldn't do anything right at school.

'Oh, Jesus, Mary and Joseph!' Gran's prayers annoyed me. I walked up to my bedroom. The sun had moved round so the room was in shadow. Lying on my bed, I put my hands over my face and tried to blot out all that had happened.

I lay on my bed for hours and cried. I still felt cold and alone. My nose and the back of my throat hurt with a kind of dryness. So did my head. It sort of pounded.

14
I CAN'T FACE SCHOOL

Dagenham

Wednesday

Dear Patrick

I tried to phone you last night, but the line was engaged all evening. Perhaps your mother was busy making lots of calls - keeping British Telecom shareholders in their finery, no doubt.

First of all, I want you to know that I love you and care about you more than anything. I wish we were still living in the same house, but that's not possible. Anyway, our Saturdays together are always good. We probably spend more time together than some of these top businessmen spend with their sons - and they live in the same house.

It's been very lonely for me since I left, even though I've been living with Gran and Grandad. A few weeks ago I met a young woman, Gemma, who has been very kind and helpful. She is a youth and community worker, like myself, so we have a lot in common. When I finish on the course today I will be moving into Gemma's flat. She has a spare room and it will help her financially if she has a lodger. I think it will be good for me too. I'm a bit old to be living with my 'mummy and daddy'!

Next Saturday we'll meet up – I'll go across to Dagenham, to your gran's. If you like we can meet up with Gemma later in the day. It's up to you. You'll like her; she's a lovely person.

I'll probably see you tomorrow evening, at the meeting in school, or Saturday. It's best if we don't discuss this in front of your mum. It might upset her – she's a bit fragile at the moment.

Keep smiling, Patrick.

Dad

Dagenham

Wednesday

Kate

I will be able to make the meeting tomorrow. We need to encourage Patrick to choose the right subjects – especially if things aren't going well for him at school.

Sorry – I won't be able to go for a drink afterwards. I had made arrangements before I received your letter. As it is, I can only just make the meeting – hopefully it won't last too long.

I'm moving out of my parents' place. I'll be sharing a flat in Forest Gate with one of my colleagues, Gemma. She's got a spare room – it will help with her bills and the mortgage. If Patrick wants to see my place, he can – but only with your permission.

Glad you enjoyed the 'old' country. Now it's back to reality!

See you tomorrow. Sean

Thursday morning. The sun woke me again, really early. Mum and I ate breakfast together, in silence – well, quietly at first. I was glad; my head still ached.

'I've heard it all now!' My mother, shouting, walked up and down the kitchen, reading the letter from my dad. I'd received one too, but we didn't stop and compare.

'I suppose he's sleeping in the spare room. That's just for public consumption, Patrick.' She thumped the letter furiously.

'Can I still see Dad on Saturday?'

'No!' Her answer was loud, final and uncompromising.

'Why not?'

She just looked at me with a mixture of impatience and anger. She searched for an excuse. 'I don't know, I just don't want you to see him . . . not at the moment, anyway.'

'Why, Mum?' I asked again, politely and quietly.

'*Because*, that's why. There doesn't need to be a reason. I just said no and that's enough. You don't have to have a reason for everything.'

'But you've always said . . .' I was just about to challenge her, when she interrupted me again.

'Never mind what I've always said . . . Things are different now. Don't ask me to be reasonable, Patrick, because I can't be. Not at the moment, anyway.' And, after a pause, 'Go and get yourself sorted out for school.'

This was always the way with my mum – one minute she was telling me to behave more grown up and the next minute she spoke to me like I was a three-year-old. Adults can be so hypocritical at times. They tell you to behave, be kind and have respect for people, then they treat you like a piece of stale, mouldy cake. Suddenly I remembered what had happened yesterday. 'Mum, I can't go to school today.'

'What do you mean, you can't?' She was still impatient and angry.

'After what happened yesterday. I just can't face it. Can I take the day off?'

'No. I can't face going to work, but we need to eat. Go and get yourself ready. Stop being so difficult.' Now she wasn't even looking at me.

'Mum, I don't feel too good.'

'What's up with you?'

'I feel . . . well, I've had a headache for about two days and I can't concentrate properly.'

'So have I. It's better to go and face up to things.' She rearranged a few things in the kitchen and went out. It's a good job I wasn't dying. She'd probably tell me to wipe the blood off the kitchen floor.

Lansbury Gardens

Wednesday night

Dear Sister Mary Rita

Thanks for your note. Patrick won't tell me much about what happened at school today. I think he's very upset, well, we're all very upset about what is happening here at the moment. Sean, Patrick's father, has met another woman and has moved in with her. I honestly didn't think it would come to this. In fact, I thought we might be close to a reconciliation. It's difficult for us to concentrate on anything - this just seems like such a major hurdle.

Patrick is very reluctant to go to school tomorrow. He says he's not well. I don't want to take him to the doctor in case he's prescribed tranquillizers. I wouldn't want him to get addicted to them at such an early age.

To be honest, I don't know what to do. I can't cope myself, never mind about having to cope with Patrick too. Sean's mother has been very good to us, though she is alarmed at Patrick's reaction to events. He is being very melodramatic. I feel he may be overreacting just to get the attention.

I'll send him into school tomorrow and, hopefully, he will have recovered from the upset. We'll be at the meeting tomorrow evening and, if Sean leaves promptly after our appointment, then I may have a chance to have a brief word with you.

Thanks again for all your support.

Kate Connolly

15

TRUANTING

I didn't go to school. I didn't want to see anyone, not even Dixon or Dunny. After I'd got ready I walked it into town. The library opened at half-eight. The librarian eyed me suspiciously, but I convinced her that I had to do some research for my history. The papers were all being read by men whose jackets smelt of egg and chips – as if they'd hung them up at the back of their cookers.

After my 'research' I wandered over to the shopping arcade. It was like a youth club; the 'Truanters' or 'Bunkers' Union of Langdon met here every day. Swapping benches and smoking, they watched shoppers arguing over the prices in Mothercare and discussing where they should eat lunch.

I stood a safe distance away from the benches, watching the security guards moving a crowd of reluctant teenagers. They were like demonstrators – floppy, yet resistant. Their arms hung back as the security guards threatened to radio for the police. The Bunkers laughed hilariously and shouted, 'I'm scared,' with sarcasm borrowed from their teachers.

It was safer still in the computer department of Allders. Before long a woman dressed in the store uniform pounced on me and asked suspiciously, 'Shouldn't you be at school?'

'I'm waiting for my mum. I've got a dental

appointment.' I'd heard them say it on the benches outside. She walked away.

'Do you like cider?' It was a boy about the same age as me, from the school next to ours. He sort of half spoke whilst he was absorbed in a computer game. It was a bit frustrating on the machines – they only gave you a taster of each game. I suppose it was to stop people like me spending all day playing with the computers they were trying to sell.

'It's all right,' I lied. I'd never tasted cider. My mum was quite strict about me drinking alcohol. We never kept much in the house – her grandfather had been an alcoholic, so she said she had an inherent wariness of the stuff. There were always bottles of sherry and whisky in the cupboard for Christmas. My dad said that it was very inhospitable not to have drink in the house. He liked to stock up just before Christmas and other important events. There was always a row about it. Dad said Mum was infecting us with her paranoia.

'You got any dinner money?' It was the boy on the computer again.

'Yes, why?'

'Want to get a bottle of cider?' He turned and looked at me, rattling the dinner money in his blazer pocket.

'I can't,' I lied again. I felt uncomfortable. This boy who I didn't really know asking me if I'd share a bottle of cider. He'd probably take my money and then run off with the bottle. 'I'm meeting my dad in a minute.'

'You chicken!' He looked at me with contempt

and disgust. As he walked out of Allders he kicked me deliberately on my shin. Then he waved two grubby fingers at me and shouted, 'You poofter! You're just a mummy's boy!'

I wasn't. My mum didn't have any time for me.

I walked back through the shopping centre. The idea of a cold bottle of cider was appealing – I'd buy a bottle, sit in the park near town, and sunbathe. It was a lovely July day.

Little notices described the wine: Fruity – suitable for fish dishes. Then above that was a caution: We do not serve alcohol to anyone under eighteen years of age. I rolled my school jumper up and put my school tie in my pocket. Looking like a young office-worker I approached the checkout. Nervously I placed the cider on the moving belt. The cashier didn't even cast a glance in my direction. She was tired and unhappy, pausing only to push the glasses up her nose as the sweat allowed them to inch away from her eyes.

It was quiet in the supermarket. As I walked away I heard another cashier say, 'He weren't eighteen, Elaine. You want to be careful.'

Elaine didn't say anything. She was tired and unhappy and her glasses were getting on her nerves. It was too late, anyway. In a few minutes I'd be in the park, lying in the sun, drinking a bottle of cold, refreshing cider.

I thought cider would taste like Coke or lemonade – sweet and fizzy – but it didn't. It had a sort of dry taste. Every mouthful I took made me so thirsty I felt like I had to drink more. As well as tasting dry it also had a sickly, bittersweet taste. How could anyone get addicted to alcohol when it tasted so awful? After a while my head began to swim.

I was sitting on one of the artificial hills overlooking the town. From here I could see the buildings in the town centre, and the new redbrick magistrates court. The shops, flats and offices started to separate and wander off in different directions. I closed my eyes. Something played a tune in my head, moving down to the back of my eyes, reaching eventually to my eyelids, which twitched with the uncertainty of the very tired.

I lay back. That was better. The bottle fell from my hand and rolled down the hill. I hadn't drunk all of it, but I'd had enough. I didn't know what was happening – at the bottom of the hill somebody tutted. In a strange way I felt very happy and I wondered why I was even bothered about my mum and dad. Why did I worry about school? No hassle. I could go in tomorrow and face them all. I could tell Murphy what to do with his assignments.

It was a good job that I'd taken the day off. Well, tomorrow . . . I tried to say the word tomorrow – the syllables all fell in the wrong order: 'Motommor', 'Worottom', 'Ommotrow'. Thinking about saying tomorrow, I fell asleep.

When I awoke, Murphy and my mum and dad were all inside my head arguing, thumping on the sides of my skull and trying to escape. I was lying by the side of the park gates, close to the walking feet of people taking short cuts through the park on their way home. As they passed me their voices were hushed, almost as a mark of disgust.

It was hard to focus. I was frightened because my mind was in such a jumble. Why was I lying here? Then it began to dawn on me – school, English assignments, truanting and cider. The happiness I had felt just a short while ago had evaporated. It had escaped whilst I slept. Now I had to face my mother with a headache and a creased shirt, stained with grass.

The thought of running away to Forest Gate to talk to my dad came to my mind, but then I thought of the flamenco woman. My dad wouldn't be there anyway. He'd be at work. He was coming to the meeting at school. The meeting – I had to be there too. It was hard to communicate the panic to my back and legs; they didn't seem to be working all that well.

Somehow I managed to stand and walk home. With any luck, Mum would be so preoccupied she wouldn't notice that my face didn't fit together any more and my legs seemed to have ideas of their own.

I really, really wanted to run away, but I hated the idea of ending up begging for a living in the middle of Hungerford Bridge; spending my days looking down towards St Paul's, pausing only for coffee in a café where they weren't fussy about their customers. Then again, it might be easier than facing my mum in her present state.

All the way home I practised saying tomorrow. The syllables fell together. Maybe she wouldn't notice my clothes.

Sister Mary Rita sat in our living-room, across the table from my mum. I thought it was just part of the dream where Murphy had been trying to pull my work out of my head. It wasn't.

They spoke, Mum first. 'Hello, Patrick, how are you?' So kind and gentle – it was only to impress Sister.

'Hello, Mum. Hello, Sister.' I nodded my head towards Sister – it came out like a bow at the end of a performance. It felt like it – this was such hard work.

'Evening, Patrick. Had a good day?' Sister Mary Rita's look said everything. She knew I hadn't been in school. She had just come to report me.

'Yes, lovely.' I didn't look at her. I wasn't good at telling lies, but I'd seen my mum look past me or at the buttons on my shirt when *she* wasn't telling the truth. 'I'm just going upstairs. What time do we need to leave, Mum?'

'What for?'

'For my options meeting.' I spoke the words slowly and carefully.

'I'll give you a shout when I'm ready, Patrick.' This was a bit much to take. It's very hard when your mother has a split personality – especially when I mostly see the nasty side of that split.

I went upstairs and closed my eyes. My back felt

sore after lying on the ground for so many hours. Then, minutes later – well, it could have been hours or days – my mum said it was time to leave.

24 Lansbury Gardens
Langdon
Essex

4 July

Dear Sarah

I just wanted to write and say thanks for your hospitality during our few days in Cork. It was a lovely break, which certainly helped myself and Patrick. Thanks for all your help with Patrick; he's really getting down to his English assignment. You inspired him, Sarah.

I wish that I could say that it's nice to be back. As you probably gathered, Sean and I have been through a difficult patch in recent months. In fact, Sean moved out to live with his parents - we both thought that it would be a good thing. However, earlier on this week I discovered that Sean is living with another woman. These last few days have been very difficult. Patrick has taken the news badly, although I think he may be overreacting. He was already having difficulties with his schoolwork - funnily enough, he was beginning to be enthusiastic about his work again after his holiday. Now this.

I thought of Sean so much at the novena service in Cork and I prayed that there would be a reconciliation. Patrick finds it so difficult to cope with us living apart.

I've had to take some time off work today as Patrick has truanted - the first time ever in almost three years at secondary school. One of his teachers, Sister Mary Rita, has been very helpful. She has advised me to play down his behaviour at present. It's very hard. Patrick won't talk to me about the situation, so it's almost impossible to work out what he's really thinking.

Thanks again for your kindness to us last week.

Love

Kate

16

PARENTS' EVENING

I am never, ever going back to school again. I will throw myself in front of a lorry on the M25 before I go back to school. Another thing – I don't want to see my dad again. Or his fancy flamenco woman. Never again. I don't like living with my mum, either. They brought me up to be good, not to be selfish, be kind and to share everything. Well, the only thing they share is misery and unhappiness. They're so selfish – to think I used to like them. They are so selfish. They really showed me up at the meeting.

Just as we were about to sit at Miss Brodie's desk to talk about my subject options, my dad turned up. Miss Brodie was running about fifteen minutes late, so me and Mum thought Dad wasn't coming. Then he turned up. He walked through the door, holding this woman's hand. As soon as he saw me looking over he let go of the woman's hand. She sat at the side of the hall whilst my dad sat beside my mum. Then it started.

'You're late!' Quiet anger just escaping from my mum's firmly closed lips.

'Sorry, I was held up. In fact . . . my car has broken down. I had to get a lift,' said Dad, smiling at Miss Brodie as if we'd all been stuck in a holiday traffic jam together.

'I thought you were just a lodger in her house.' Mum's head moved very slightly in the direction of Dad's flamenco woman.

'I am.' Still smiling at Miss Brodie, 'Shall we begin?'

'How many landladies hold hands with their lodgers and accompany them to their children's parents' evenings?' She was shouting now. Miss Brodie coughed nervously. The hall became strangely silent.

'Don't make a scene, dear . . . There was nobody else to give me a lift . . .' My dad tried to calm her.

'What?' She was almost screaming now. 'Don't make a scene? Don't make a bloody scene? You've made the scene. You turn up here with your landlady-cum-fancy woman and you tell me not to make a scene? You make me sick!' Then she hit him. Across the face. His face and neck flashed red with the pain and the shock.

Dad still looked at Miss Brodie and said in a quiet, flat voice, 'You must forgive her. She's a bit emotional at present.'

As they argued I could feel my stomach churning over. It wasn't just the cider – I'd eaten something out of the fridge that didn't taste right.

I looked at Miss Brodie. She watched in horror as her evening, planned down to the last detail, was being wrecked by a broken marriage. It wasn't just the cider or the stuff out of the fridge, it was the look on Miss Brodie's face. She looked at my parents as though they were dog muck and she'd just walked on it and trodden it into her lovely carpet. I couldn't help it – I just coughed and I vomited. It was quite violent the way that it came out – splashing all over Miss Brodie's notes and her new outfit. People jumped back as if I'd opened fire with a machine-gun. Mum and Dad stopped arguing and Mum screamed, 'Patrick!' Then she clipped me across the back of the head, even though I felt dreadful.

I can't go back. I'll never live it down. As I sat there I could smell the cider. In a haze I watched as the caretaker, who stood like a security guard at all these events, rushed around with a mop and a bucket. The whole hall stirred. As my stomach waited to empty the rest of the contents, I ran for the toilet.

I can't go back. What will Dixon and Dunny say? What will Murphy say? He probably thinks that I did it deliberately. How many detentions will I get for this act? Well, at least it stopped Mum and Dad arguing about the flamenco woman.

How could he do it? How could he bring her to the meeting? He had said it was important – he wants me to do well at school. He wants me to choose the right subjects. He wasn't even thinking about me – just himself and his flaming flamenco woman.

Thursday night

Sean

Are you satisfied? We've seen your fancy woman now! What about *Patrick*? Can't you see what you're doing to him? I thought we had agreed to do the best *for him*.

You're not seeing him this Saturday, so don't expect him!

Kate

17

THE AFTERMATH

HOLY FAMILY SCHOOL · LANGDON · ESSEX

Mrs K. Connolly
24 Lansbury Gardens
Langdon
Essex

5 July

Dear Mrs Connolly

We are most concerned about Darren's behaviour at present. As you may already have heard, on Wednesday of this week Darren was asked to read part of his life story to a group of German visitors. Halfway through reading his extract Darren appeared to have a panic attack. He left the library, without permission, then he walked through school in a most aggressive manner. Once again, he was invited to talk about his difficulties, but he was extremely rude to the teacher.

The following day Darren was absent from school. Mr Grant, the school caretaker, assures me that Darren had been drinking alcohol before yesterday's meeting and that he was sick as a result of this.

As Darren is continuing to behave in such a disturbed manner, we feel that it would be in his best interests if we referred him to the Educational Psychologist. Darren is obviously troubled at the moment and he needs expert help so that he can face up to the many things which are worrying him.

I have advised his classmates that it will be in the best interests of all concerned if no further reference is made to the events of last night (at the Consultation Evening). However, Miss Brodie-Vasquez has informed me that she intends to present Darren with a bill for the cleaning of her outfit. It was, as you may have gathered, a brand-new outfit. If there are any difficulties over the payment of this bill, please contact myself rather than Miss Brodie-Vasquez.

If you are in agreement with our suggestion that Darren should see the Educational Psychologist, please consult the school as soon as possible. We hope to see Darren back in school on Monday.

We look forward to hearing from you.

Yours sincerely

J. J. Murphy

J.J.Murphy
Deputy Headteacher

It was almost eleven o'clock when I woke. It didn't matter. I wasn't going to school. It seemed strange – for the first time in ages my mum hadn't said goodbye before she went to work. Maybe she'd left me, gone to find Dad and the flamenco woman. Maybe she hadn't gone to work.

Gran bustled into the room. 'Here's some toast and tea for youself. Now, when you've had that, get yourself ready. Then me and you are going to have a really good talk. There's been enough of this nonsense, Patrick Connolly.'

'Morning, Gran,' I replied. She smiled because she knows how funny I think she is when she doesn't say hello properly.

'D'you know your trouble, Patrick?' my gran asked, whilst searching my face for an answer. 'You don't know anything about your mother and father. Sure they're too busy with their own lives to be worrying about you. Isn't that an awful thing?'

I nodded – it was true. My mum and dad didn't seem to bother much about me any more.

'Would you like me to tell you some more about your mum and dad, Patrick?'

We talked for a long while. Gran told me about my dad's schooldays and then about how my mum and dad met. The feeling of sickness had gone from me and it was Friday.

My Life Story

PART FOUR

My dad grew up in a very close-knit Irish community in Dagenham. His family lived close to the church, so their life revolved around the parish and the parish club.

My grandparents were very popular and well-known in their area and so when my dad was born everybody made a big fuss of him. My dad was delighted when his two sisters were born. He always helped my granny to change their nappies and play with them. My grandad didn't like this, as he said that it wasn't right for little boys to help their mothers too much. He thought that my dad would grow up with 'funny ideas'. Despite this, my gran insisted on Dad helping with the housework when he was nine. The job he hated more than any other was washing the potatoes.

When he was eleven my dad went to a Catholic secondary school. It was very strict, so Dad got into a lot of trouble. When he was in the fourth year at school he was caught smoking behind the woodwork room. My gran was so upset. She thought that he might turn into a juvenile delinquent. She says that she prayed for him a great deal and it worked. In his fifth year at school my dad settled down and worked hard for his exams.

My mum and dad were members of their parish youth club and this club always organized good outings during the summer holidays. One Sunday they went to Southend. My dad went with all of his mates and my mum went with her friend, Carole. Dad and his mates sat at the back of the coach making a lot of noise, so my mum told them to grow up and behave. (The whole youth club had been told that there would be no more outings if people were silly on the coach.)

My mum thought that my dad was a hooligan, and when he tried to talk to her she was very snooty. This hurt my dad because he really liked my mum – he thought she was very pretty, and deep down he wasn't a hooligan. He was just showing off in front of all his mates.

When my dad started his apprenticeship at Ford's he used to see my mum catching the bus to school (she was in the sixth form). Before long he gave up the idea of going out with her because she seemed too confident and he was quite shy. Mum wasn't really confident; it was her way of showing off in front of her friends and the nuns. So Dad started going out with other girls. Every other Saturday he went to watch West Ham play at home. He didn't enjoy it a lot of the time, but all his mates went, so he just tagged along.

My mum and dad eventually met again about two years later in a chip shop in Dagenham. My dad still liked my mum even though he'd been out with lots of girls in the mean time. Mum was impressed with the way Dad had changed, so they started going out together. By this time Mum was at college in Manchester, training to be a teacher, so they only met up during the holidays.

My mum's parents didn't like her going out with my dad, as he was only a Ford's apprentice then. They wanted her to marry a doctor or an accountant or even a teacher, as they felt that they'd spent a lot of money on her education. A lot of the time they tried to talk her out of meeting up with my dad. It was hard for my mum as she loved her parents, but she also liked my dad a great deal.

When they had been going out together about six months my mum discovered that she was pregnant. Her parents were absolutely furious and suggested that she should go to live in another town until she had the baby and then give it up for adoption. Then she would be able to continue her college career. They didn't want to talk to my dad, as they thought he had wrecked my mum's life.

Eventually Mum and Dad decided to get married. They had a small wedding with just immediate family, but my mum's mother wouldn't come to the church. In fact, my mum and her mother hardly spoke for years after my mum decided to marry my dad. My grandma thought that Mum and Dad had brought shame on the family. We never really see my mum's mother now.

Four months after they got married, I was born. My mother and father wanted to call me Darren because they liked it and, at the time, it was a fashionable name. Then, the day before the christening, my grandmother objected to my name. She said it wasn't a proper Christian name and that my parents were acting like heathens calling me such a name. She also said that the priest wouldn't baptize me if I was called Darren. So at the last minute my parents added the name Patrick, to please my grandmother.

END OF PART FOUR

Forest Gate

Friday

Dear Patrick

Your mother and I have a lot of explaining to do. I don't think we'll be able to meet up on Saturday. I'm sure your mother has her reasons. Perhaps you're still suffering from the stomach bug which hit you yesterday. Have you recovered from that yet? I hope so. Don't go back to school until you're completely better. Did you eat something which made you ill or is it one of those things that's going around?

I rang Mr Murphy at school today and apologized for your mother's behaviour. I don't know what is coming over her - she was never like that. Mr Murphy said that it will take Miss Brodie-Vasquez a couple of weeks to get all the forms sorted out for the subject options, so things won't be as well organized as they were in past years. Mr Murphy told me that you might need some extra support at school. We'll talk about this again.

I'm sorry that things have turned out this way, Patrick. A few months ago your mother said that she was tired of me and tired of being married. She suggested that we should have a trial separation. To be fair to your mother, she offered to move out. She had even arranged a place to stay in Barking. I said that I thought she should stay, so I went to Gran and Grandad's.

It hurt me so much, the way things had turned out, and my colleagues (workmates) were very helpful. Gemma, in particular, was outstanding. Her support has really kept me going in recent months. I won't say too much more about that. I'd like you to meet her as soon as possible and make your own judgements about her.

As I said before, I didn't want all this to happen. But it has happened and we must make the best of it. I'll ring you on Sunday or Monday and we'll try to arrange to meet.

Don't forget, I still love you and care about you. Look after your mum.

Dad

Forest Gate

Friday

Kate

Only a few days ago you wrote: Whatever happens, we must never stop talking about our son. He comes first.

In your jealous rage did you remember those words? I think you owe Patrick a huge apology.

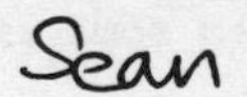

18
SATURDAY

There wasn't a sound in the house and nothing good on television as it was summer. I went to the park. I took an old plastic ball and practised shooting at the red brick wall with the white markings for a goalpost. I wished Dixon and Dunny were there with the leather football, then I remembered that Dixon was acting with his drama group on Saturdays. Dunny plays for a Saturday league team. In the afternoon he works in a florist's in town, selling off the fresh flowers so they won't die in the shop on Sunday.

It was difficult to have a decent game with myself – if I hit the ball too fiercely against the wall it bounced off in a different direction. A young couple pushed a child in a swing. They laughed and the child chuckled.

'Shall we go for a walk, Patrick?' Mum asked as soon as I walked in the house. She didn't look at me, she stared at the suds in the sink, wrapping them around her hands as she spoke. It wasn't my idea of an exciting Saturday.

'Do we have to?'

'No . . . we don't have to, but I think we should. You know, just to clear the air.' She still looked at the suds, just throwing a quick, sidelong glance to see if I was still there.

'Oh . . . OK.' Talking to my mum was getting to be like school – I didn't want to, but it was sort of compulsory. I didn't really have much choice.

Just over the sea-wall at Canvey there's a little hut that sells tea, cakes, ice-cream and sweets. My mum bought me a cup of tea and a cake. We sat sipping our tea and looking out over the Thames estuary. It was warm and very bright; the water sort of glistened in the July heat. On the beach people paddled – a health scare stopped them committing their whole bodies to the salt water.

'I'm sorry, Pat.' She still didn't look at me, but watched a ship moving along the centre of the river, led by a smaller boat.

'It's all right.' What else could I say?

'No, it isn't all right. I'll never be able to forgive myself for what happened on Thursday evening. But . . . your dad provoked me . . . bringing that woman along . . . I was so humiliated.'

'I can't ever go back to school, Mum.' I said it quietly and confidently, expecting her to agree and then talk about where I could go for the final two years of my schooling.

'Don't be silly, Patrick. It's not that serious.' She was half smiling. It made me furious.

'Don't be *silly*? I can't go back and face Murphy and Brodie-Vases or whatever she's called. I feel so stupid. You and Dad were fighting with one another, I was sick over all the option documents and everybody in that big hall was watching us, and you say, Don't be silly?'

'I know, I know I did a terrible thing. I was so

full of anger and jealousy. It's . . . very difficult to explain.' She looked out at the river again. Windsurfers and jet-skiers seemed to breeze across our view. 'All I can really say is . . . I'm sorry. I wish your dad hadn't brought that woman. I wish I hadn't reacted the way that I did, but it has happened. Do you know, Patrick . . .' A long pause as she bit back the tears and tried to appear composed. 'I think I was angry with myself on Thursday evening, and part of the reason I shouted was because . . . well . . . I was sort of shouting at myself. Do you understand?'

'No.' I didn't. I really didn't understand what she was saying.

'Well, it's hard for me to say this, but it's all my fault, you know. I started all this. I am responsible and that's why I'm so sorry.' She looked straight at me, as she did many years ago when she told me there was no tooth fairy or Santa Claus. 'Dad would probably still be at home if it wasn't for me. He certainly wouldn't be living with another woman.' It was strange seeing my mum like this. She had never talked to me in this way before. It was almost as though somebody had told her that she had to do this.

'Why are you telling me this, Mum?'

'Because I'm frightened of what might happen to you if I don't start telling you the truth.' Her voice shook as she spoke.

'What do you mean?'

As I asked, Mum stood up and gestured to me to do the same. We walked along the narrow promenade, past couples walking their dogs and families all linked up and happy. Mum looked away from people we passed, and behind her dark glasses the tears rolled down her face.

'It's a long story, but I'll try and tell you.' She wiped her eyes, blew her nose and cleared her throat.

Some of it I already knew. Gran had told me yesterday so that I could finish off my life story. My mum told me about her giving up college and not working for years. Then she said she didn't have any decent qualifications.

'So . . . when your dad was given the opportunity to go back to college five years ago, I was really jealous.'

'Why, Mum?'

'I don't know. I felt as though it was his fault that I'd had to give up college all those years ago. Well, anyway . . . your dad and I never talked about it. He'd come home and do his studies and I felt sort of . . . shut out. Then he got this marvellous job. And what am I doing? Working in a dead-end job!'

'I thought you liked your job.'

'I do, but I could be doing . . . so much better, if only . . .'

'If only I hadn't been born!' It was all becoming clear to me. I got in the way of my mum's education many years ago and she hadn't really forgiven me.

'No!' she shouted at me. Families walking by stopped to see why she was shouting. She smiled at them and continued in a quieter voice, 'No, I don't mean that.'

'Dad said you wanted to leave a few months ago, Mum. Why did you want to leave?' I felt as though I was standing on a crumbling pile of sand. In a minute a wave would wash it away and I would be left stranded.

'Sean had no right to tell you that. It was private. We had an argument. I thought I couldn't live under the same roof as him. He was just driving me up the wall all the time. I didn't want to throw him out, so I said I would go.'

'Would you have left me?' My voice started out strong, but it became a high-pitched cry.

She didn't answer for a long time. Then, in a voice broken with tears and sadness, 'Oh, Patrick, we've been so selfish. We only thought of ourselves. I thought you would be able to cope no matter what happened, no matter who was at home. Your dad loves you so much, you know. I'm so sorry, Patrick.' She sat down at the edge of the pathway, with her legs dangling over the side. I watched her sobs take over. The families slowed down as they passed; one or two women asked me if she was all right. I stood back, lonely and embarrassed, praying that none of my class would walk past.

'I gave up my education and my career for your dad. I sacrificed my family for Sean. They begged me not to marry him and then they forgot that I existed when we married. Now here I am – no career, no family, no husband!'

I wanted to tell her that I was her family, but she seemed to be past any consolation. She just put her head down on her knees and cried. She wasn't crying for me – the tears were all for herself. I wanted to cry too, but I'm nearly fourteen; I'm nearly a man and men aren't supposed to cry.

24 Lansbury Gardens
Langdon
Essex

6 July

Dear Mr Murphy

Thank you for your letter. I would rather Patrick didn't see the Educational Psychologist. There are no deep-rooted reasons for Patrick's 'disturbed' behaviour. He has had to cope with his parents' marriage breakdown, as well as other problems we've had at home in recent months. It is up to Patrick's father and myself to face up to these problems and help Patrick through this difficult time.

I think Patrick's problems were worsened because he had to write his life story at such a delicate time in his life. It would have been better if Patrick had been able to do this assignment in a few months' time, when things are calmer.

I would like to apologize for disrupting the evening on Thursday and I would also like to say that I am grateful for your sensitivity in dealing with Patrick's classmates, concerning his sickness.

Hopefully, the last two weeks of term will pass without event. If there are any problems please ring me at my work number.

Yours sincerely

Kathleen Connolly

Kathleen Connolly

19

DIXON'S NEWS

Dixon rang me on Satuday afternoon. It's not his style – he doesn't normally ring me. He said the way things were going I'd soon be able to join his Saturday drama group.

'I'm not going back to school again.' I spoke with the seriousness of one who would never change his mind.

'Why not? 'Cause of what happened?' Dixon sounded as though he couldn't believe it. He didn't wait for my reply. 'Don't be so daft. I've known lads mess themselves in class one day and come into school the next day wearing jeans. Everyone knew why their school trousers were being washed, but nobody said anything.'

'Yes . . . but this is different,' I struggled on.

'Don't be daft. You're not special just 'cause you spewed all over Brodie-Vasquez, you know. I think you've got a lot of bottle, Damp Proof Course!' Dixon laughed.

'I didn't do it on purpose – it just came out.' Dixon laughed even more. 'I'm not going back . . .'

'Murphy said no one was to talk about your problem. He says if he hears anyone mentioning it they'll get an after-school. Dunny said he overhead Brodie-Vasquez saying she's going to sue you!' Now he laughed heartily. 'You've got to join our drama group. There aren't many people who can do what you did!'

The idea appealed to me, but Saturday was the day for my dad. Well, it used to be. 'I'll think about it. I normally see my dad on Saturday mornings; I'll see what he says.'

'Is your dad still living?' Dixon was quite serious, but there was also a touch of sympathy in his voice.

'Yes . . . it was awful, wasn't it?'

'No . . . just good drama. What was it all about?'

'All sorts. I can't say much as my mum might come in and she'd kill me if she knew I'd been telling anyone about what's happening.'

'I like your parents.' Dixon wasn't being sarcastic. I wanted to like them too, but I didn't at the moment.

'When do we get our option choices for the next year?'

'Not till the end of this week. We've all got to have another interview with Brodie-Vasquez.'

'Oh God, no!' I think the memory might make me vomit again.

'Look, I've got to go. Rehearsal – we're doing a play, in the Towngate Studio during the holidays. See you Monday, D.P.C.?'

'Yes, suppose so . . . Thanks for calling.'

I was pleased Dixon had called. Things weren't as horrific as I thought they might be. Apart from Brodie-Vasquez hating me. Well, at least she wouldn't make me sit in her office any more. Hopefully, it might stop her from being so nosy.

Maybe I will go back to school after all.

24 Lansbury Gardens
Langdon

7 July

Dear Sister Mary Rita

I just wanted to thank you for taking time to listen to me on Thursday. You were a great help to me in my darkest hour. Although I have many friends, I feel, at the moment, as though I have no one to turn to. They are Sean's friends too and they think that I have brought all this on myself. They wouldn't give me a favourable hearing. Thanks again for your kindness to me.

Patrick and I talked yesterday. I wish I could say that we have everything sorted out, but we haven't. Patrick is feeling incredibly insecure at the moment and it will take a miracle to make him feel confident and happy again. However, I think he will go back to school on Monday. As the days pass he's beginning to put things into perspective. Could you continue to watch over him at school and if you think he's truanting please ring me at my work number. I can't afford to take any more time off at the moment or I could find myself unemployed by September. I remember you said that I had to get my priorities right - well, two of my main priorities are to pay the mortgage and to buy food. It looks as though Sean won't be able to support us for much longer and, as it is, he doesn't pay a great deal anyway. I have to work, both for financial reasons and for my sanity.

Thanks again for your advice and support.

Kathleen Connolly

'You know what I think? Patrick is the only one amongst ye with any sense! That's what I think.' It was Gran. She had arrived with Grandad on Sunday afternoon. She walked in through the back gate. It was a warm day; Mum was lying on a blanket reading. I sat at the white plastic table doing some maths homework. It was typical of Gran. She never said hello.

'Good afternoon, Gran.' Mum spoke as if correcting my gran. I thought it was funny how she called her 'Gran' when she wasn't her gran. Still, I suppose 'Mother-in-law' is a bit of a mouthful. 'So . . . you must have heard.'

''Course I heard. Everyone in that blessed school has a relation in Dagenham. I'm surprised they didn't announce it at Mass this morning. I don't know what you two are playing at.' Gran was shouting now. Mum gestured at her to keep her voice down, but Gran didn't take any notice. 'I will not be quiet. Sure, you two want your heads banging together.'

Grandad sat beside me at the white table and lit a cigarette. 'What's that you're doing, Pat? Algebra?' He took the textbook and looked at it as if he was reading Swahili. 'That's fierce difficult!' I agreed with him and we laughed. 'Sure, what do you need that for anyway?'

'You don't. It's what school is all about, Grandad. It just makes your life more difficult.'

'Sure, Patrick, I left school at twelve and look't the typhoon I turned out to be!' He laughed.

'Do you mean ty*coon*, Grandad?'

'Indeed I do. Do you see what that little bit of education does for you, Pat? Don't be listening to me. You stick with your studies and do well. We'll have some Irish names in the government yet!'

Across the garden Gran was still giving out to my mother. Then, when she looked closely at my mum's tired, tear-stained face, she knelt down beside her and hugged her. As Grandad told me about all the losers he'd backed yesterday, I heard my gran saying to my mum, 'You're only young yet, girl. You can start again. Never mind about himself up in Forest Gate. He's made his own bed. Let yourself and Patrick get on with your own lives.' Then, as if the chapter was closed, she said, 'Do you two never do any weeding? Sure this garden's crawling with weeds and rubbish!'

My Life Story

PART FIVE

My mum and dad decided not to have any more children after I was born. This was because my mum suffered a great deal whilst she was expecting me. Also, she hoped to go back to college when I was about three or four. This didn't work out and my mum just let the years drift by. She enjoyed being a mum, but she always felt a bit disappointed – as though there was something missing.

When I was about fourteen months old I fell out of my high chair and broke my nose. My parents have some interesting photographs of me with purple bruises spreading across the middle of my face. My grandparents were horrified when this happened to me. They said that I was neglected – my dad was very cross with his mum for saying this. For a while they didn't speak.

The rest of my childhood passed without any serious incidents or accidents. Every year we went to Ireland on holiday – to Mayo, to see my dad's cousins. I have some very good memories of holidays in Ireland, although it can be quite depressing when it rains.

My first day at school was a bit of a disaster. I wasn't really used to playing with other children, so I cried a lot and my mum tells me that I found it difficult to share. I soon became used to school and I grew to like it.

I transferred to Holy Family at the age of eleven. Two years before I started at Holy Family my dad was made redundant by Ford's. He applied to do several courses and eventually he was accepted on a youth and community course. Since he started doing the course my dad has changed quite a lot. As soon as he finished the course my mum changed her job. She used to work for a small company in Langdon. Now she travels into the City every day.

In the last year there have been many changes in my life. A few months ago my parents decided to separate. I see my dad on Saturdays when he takes me out to an exhibition or to an art gallery.

At this stage I'm supposed to write about my hopes for the future. Well, the first thing is, I hope that the atmosphere in our house improves. I would like to do well at school and go to college or university. I have found it hard to concentrate in recent weeks, so I may have to forget about that particular ambition. As far as a job is concerned, I'm not too sure. I enjoy helping my gran in her garden and sometimes I think I'd like to be in charge of a large garden or work in a garden centre. I don't want to do youth work, like my dad, as it takes up too much of your time. I wouldn't want to work in the City, like my mum. People who work in the City seem to spend half their lives travelling.

I'm not too sure about things like getting

married. I know one thing though – if I ever got married and I had children I would never, ever, split up from my wife. I would always stay with her and my children, no matter what. It hurts children so much when their mums and dads split up. I know it hurts grown-ups too, but they just don't realize how children feel.

THE END

20
BACK TO SCHOOL

Dad rang on Sunday evening. Mum answered and passed the phone straight to me. 'It's someone for you,' she said in such a harsh voice.

My dad was anxious to make arrangements for the following Saturday. 'Where would you like to go, son?'

'I'm not sure. Am I allowed?'

'What do you mean, are you allowed?' He tried to be pleasant but the anger seeped through.

'You know . . .' I didn't want to say much, as the door was open and I was very conscious of Mum listening. 'After what happened . . .'

'When? What do you mean?'

'On Thursday.'

'That's up to me and your mum to sort out. Anyway, how are you feeling? Are you better?'

'Yes, I'm fine thanks, Dad.' My stomach was still churning, but it wasn't life-threatening.

'Would you like to go out somewhere next Saturday? Tell me the truth?'

'Yes . . . but with you . . . just you.' I couldn't face going out with his flamenco woman.

'Right, Pat. Well . . . I'll sort it out with your mum. Will you get her for me and we'll talk about it?'

I shouted 'Mum', then I went into the front room and listened.

'Thanks for your letter.' My mother's voice was rich with sarcasm. 'What do you mean I owe *you* an apology? . . . Why did you bring her?'

I didn't hear any more. I didn't want to listen.

My mum made the arrangements for the following Saturday. Meet up at Gran's. Forget about last Thursday. Pretend it didn't happen.

It was easier for them to forget. I had to walk through that hall every day. I had to face the teacher who sat watching them fight.

Holy Family Convent
Timberfoot Place
Langdon Newtown

8 July

Dear Kate

I was pleased to see Patrick back at school today. Although he looked nervous at times, it was most courageous of him to come back and face up to things. He has been well supported by good friends.

There is nothing that I can say that will make things any easier for you. Every family breakdown is a tragedy and only the individuals involved know the pain that is caused by careless remarks and thoughtless actions.

I'm pleased that you have decided against

Patrick seeing the Educational Psychologist - it may only increase his confusion. Life needs to be as simple as possible for Patrick at the moment.

Patrick tells me that his major English assignment is finished - it looks good and I'm sure he'll be rewarded with high marks!

If you need to talk any more, I'm here and I will listen. In the mean time, I'm praying for all of you.

God Bless Rita Keane

I never thought that being sick could make me such a hero, but it did. By the following Monday everybody had forgotten about my mum and dad, but they laughed and smiled about my 'little accident'. Miss Brodie had been giving people a lot of grief about their subject choices. She had threatened to put Dixon and Dunny into the Home Economics group. Now things had to be reorganized, thanks to me.

Murphy saw me on Monday morning. He made me feel like a patient in hospital with an infectious disease. I gave him the final parts of my life story. He said he'd mark them and write a comment before the end of the day.

In the corner of the room were the blazer and bag I'd left in the library, with the Germans. It seemed like a lifetime since I'd left them there and stood up to read my life story.

Murphy caught me looking at them and said, 'Ah yes, your things. Help yourself, Darren.' Then, after a pause, 'By the way, how are you feeling now?'

As I picked up my stuff, I said, 'Fine thanks,' and started walking to the door.

'You're not the only one, you know.' Murphy's normal voice had returned.

'What do you mean, sir?'

'There are many, many children in this school whose parents have separated, but none of them has made as much fuss as you have.'

I wanted to say something really sarcastic like, 'Thanks for telling me, sir, you've made me feel so much better,' but I didn't. I just nodded my head and tried to look full of remorse. It's like when you hurt yourself and the cut is bleeding badly and somebody says, 'That happened to me once. It hurts, doesn't it?' It doesn't stop the blood flowing or heal up the wound. All it does is make you very, very angry inside.

HOLY FAMILY SCHOOL · LANGDON · ESSEX

ENGLISH DEPARTMENT

Major Assignment

Name: Darren Patrick Connolly

Date: 8 July

Title of Assignment: My Life Story

Comment: Good. Well organized and interesting. Needs to be a little more detailed and descriptive in places. You also need to be more adventurous with your use of punctuation. Your work sometimes lacks real originality. The last section, particularly the bit about your ambition, is a bit limited and cautious. You should have been more adventurous here.

Unfortunately, we won't be able to submit this for your final year-end assessment, as you missed the assignment deadline date.

However, a reasonable effort. Consider it a practice piece.

J. J. Murphy